Congratulations. You must be proud of yourself. Yes, surely! Looking back, everyone can think of things they have achieved, fears they have overcome, actions to be proud of.

But then equally we can all look back and think of things to be ashamed of and deeds we had rather left undone.

Look at Theseus. Beauty and strength, triumphs and successes. Here and there along the way even he upset a little life like a vase of flowers. But Theseus was a hero, after all, and a hero needs a broader gangway through the world. People should step back and let him pass. For heroes are a glory in the eyes of heaven. Heroes delight the gods. Small wonder Theseus was proud.

And yet, if a hero's gifts come from the gods, what credit can he take for them? A hero should give credit where it's due and preserve a kind of modesty. Otherwise he may only be remembered by the trail of broken flowers left in his wake.

And cursed by the gods for the sin of pride.

Geraldine McCaughrean has written over a hundred books for children and adults. After many years spent working for a London publisher, she now writes full-time. Her novels have won her the Whitbread, Carnegie, Guardian, NESTA, Smarties, and Beefeater Awards. She has also written plays for stage and radio. Among her other books for Oxford University Press are *A Little Lower than the Angels*, *A Pack of Lies*, *Plundering Paradise*, *The Kite Rider*, and *Stop the Train*.

Theseus

Other books by Geraldine McCaughrean

Theseus

Geraldine McCaughrean

OXFORD
UNIVERSITY PRESS

OXFORD
UNIVERSITY PRESS

Great Clarendon Street, Oxford OX2 6DP

Oxford University Press is a department of the University of Oxford.
It furthers the University's objective of excellence in research, scholarship,
and education by publishing worldwide in

Oxford New York

Auckland Bangkok Buenos Aires
Cape Town Chennai Dar es Salaam Delhi Hong Kong Istanbul
Karachi Kolkata Kuala Lumpur Madrid Melbourne Mexico City Mumbai
Nairobi São Paulo Shanghai Taipei Tokyo Toronto

Oxford is a registered trade mark of Oxford University Press
in the UK and in certain other countries

British Library Cataloguing in Publication Data available

ISBN 0 19 274199 3

1 3 5 7 9 10 8 6 4 2

Typeset by AFS Image Setters Ltd, Glasgow

Printed in Great Britain by
Cox & Wyman Ltd, Reading, Berkshire

1

The Oracle and the Sorceress

The singers sing of a time before Theseus was born. Then, men stood like candles on the table of the earth, and their lives melted quickly away. The wild and unkempt gods roared round the world, howling and blustering like the four winds, and with little care for the men they trampled, the candles that flickered and died. A man's life was soon forgotten.

A man's memory could only be kept alive by storytellers (and the memories of storytellers are small and overcrowded) or by his own children and by their children after them . . .

King Aegeus longed for a child—a son who could keep alight his memory in the windy halls of history, and inherit the crown of Athens, too. Oh, and a son to love him, as only a son can love his father!

But Aegeus had married once and his wife had died. He had married again, but after a time, his second wife, with her narrow waist and narrow eyes looked at him and shrugged. 'The gods clearly don't mean us to have children, my dear.'

Day after night he prayed to the gods for the gift of a

1

son. But still the only sound in his courtyard and streets was of other people's children, other people's sons. Without warning, without a word, King Aegeus got up one day and left Athens in a chariot, bound for Delphi.

There, where the earth had cracked open a little like lips cracked by the wind, wisps of smoke from the Underworld leaked out into a cave. The smoke was a sickly yellow. The smell was an acrid ache in the nose—a headache—a dizziness—a clouding of the brain. For carried in the fumes were words and numbers, nightmares and dreams. They stung the eyes. They muddled the brain.

Within the swirling smoke, seated on a three-legged bronze platform higher than a man's head, a girl sat rocking to and fro. Her head rolled on her shoulders and her eyes rolled in her head. And out of her mouth fell words as wild as nonsense. This was the Delphic Oracle, doomed by her gift of prophecy to sit in the foul vapours of the Underworld with a head full of visions. This was Xenoclea-Who-Knows-All-That-Was-And-Is-And-Will-Be. Her lids were shut. But inside her head lay all the answers to every question, and far more than Man dared to ask.

The floor was trodden hollow and the step in front of the tripod was pitted where a thousand knees had knelt. For a man could come to the Oracle and ask for knowledge only the gods should know. And the Oracle could see, with her closed eyes, clear into the future.

Aegeus, when he reached the door of the temple, almost turned on his heel and left. He had been so certain on his journey, so sure of his reason for coming. Here he might have an answer to the question that bored through his pillow each night to lodge in his brain. But now he wondered.

'They all hesitate,' said a voice from inside the temple. 'They all come as far as the door and wonder, ''Would I rather not know?" You are right, King Aegeus. For all the good it will do you, you would do better not to ask, not to know.'

But Aegeus shook himself like a dog and ducked inside the doorway. 'Of course I must know! I'm a king, and unless I know, how shall I make plans for Athens? Will I ever . . . shall I ever . . . '

'Have a son? Ah, how many times have I heard that question? I am bored with it. Profoundly, boundlessly bored. Before I heard you coming, I saw your question written in the air. "Will I have a son?" The world's air is stale with that kind of question. "Will I have a child? Will I have a husband? Will I have a crown?" But *you*, Aegeus, *you* have a choice.'

'A choice? I don't want a choice, I want a son!' cried Aegeus, overbalancing off his knees so that his hands splattered the floor, wet with holy libations.

The tone of the Oracle's voice never changed. She did not even know what words spilled from her drooping, open mouth. Even childless kings could not move her to pity. 'The Sorceress Medea can give you the magic. But beware. Listen to my words, O foolish king, and let Theseus remain unborn. Accept the fate of the gods and do not bring yourself unhappiness.'

The king stumbled out of the cave, wiping his face with his dripping hands. His head was full of reechy smoke. His heart was jumping with amazement. But all the warnings rolled away and were lost. His brain was full of the name Theseus—'Theseus. Theseus! My son, Theseus!' he said, and knotting the long reins of his chariot around his waist, he whipped up his horses to a gallop.

It was all his outriders could do to catch up with him. 'To Athens, my lord? Not this road for Athens, surely?'

3

'No! To Corinth! I must see Medea the Sorceress.'

For the magic of a son, Aegeus would have ridden to the pit of the sea and prised it from the tendrils of an octopus. He would not have cared if the Sorceress Medea lived in the heart of a volcano and was as ugly as a sloth. Aegeus had never seen her and he was prepared for almost any sight—except for the one he saw.

Medea lived in a tower of pink stone, and her hair was braided with silver. Her white gown was tinged with the colours of sunset, and her hands were as white as the long wing pinions of a flying swan. She greeted Aegeus as though all her life had been spent waiting for him, and she gave him cakes and perfumed wine and the marinaded meat of turtle doves.

'And what service can I do my lord Aegeus to bring him joy?'

The king asked at once for the magic that would give him a son and heir. 'I have a thousand pieces of gold to pay you with, but if you need more I can pay you in yearly tributes of cattle and sheep and white ground flour.'

Medea held up her hand and smiled. 'You are welcome to my magic, my lord—more than welcome. All I ask is a welcome in your house if ever I should come to Athens. Now—show me yourself.'

Aegeus shuffled his feet awkwardly, spread his arms and looked down at the floor, blushing. He felt a shabby sort of a king, traipsing his dirt into the rosy drapery of her chamber. His sandals were white with dust. His tunic was sweaty. His breastplate was covered in fingermarks. Suddenly he leapt backwards as she flung a chalice of wine against his chest. It trickled down his armour, through his clothing, and dripped off his large knee-caps.

'Listen, King Aegeus, the very next time you hold a

4

woman in your arms, she will bear you a son,' said Medea softly.

'Oh, Medea! Oh, thank you! Thank you! I'm so very sorry—I'm dripping on your rug,' he said. Indeed he was not sorry; he would willingly have stood and dripped on her rug for ever. Because the longer he looked at Medea, the more beautiful she seemed. His body leaned forward from the ankles, his hands lifted from his side. He took one step towards her. Surely, one kiss was no more than he owed her for the favour she had granted him.

Medea, too, spread her arms, welcoming. Her fingers touched his . . .

Outside there was a clatter of metal against stone. The king's outriders burst into the room.

'Your chariot, my lord!'

'The horses are bolting!'

'We couldn't hold them, sir. They're out of hand!'

Aegeus ran outside to quieten his horses: they steadied at once, at the sound of his voice, and stood stock still while he wound their long reins once more round his waist. Medea came to the door to wave the king farewell. She was frowning a little.

In his longing to be home—to take his wife in his arms and give her a son—he whipped up the horses and left Medea's pink tower far behind him, dirtied by his flying dust. The sorceress, before she turned to go back inside, stamped her foot angrily and spat on the parched ground. She had meant that son to be hers.

It was a long journey from Corinth to Athens—too far by far to travel in one day. Aegeus decided to stay the night at the house of an old friend, in the village of Troezen. He was happy to the point of foolishness, hugging the servants

5

and throwing his arms round his friend. 'Do you know what, Pittheus? Shall I tell you the most wonderful thing? No, it would be wrong to speak of it. My wife must be the first to know! Great news, though, Pittheus! The greatest news of all! The greatest news for Attica since that young bear Hercules was born! Hello, who's this young beauty?' Pittheus's daughter, Aethra, was standing at his elbow with a jug to refill his goblet of wine. 'Is it really little Aethra? By the gods, you've grown! Pittheus, she's *beautiful*! Have you found a good husband for her yet?'

Aethra blushed and hurried away to fetch more food to table, and while the wine flowed and Aegeus's hands waved as he sprawled in his chair and drew great cheerful shapes in the air with his cup of wine, the beautiful young Aethra watched the king through long, lowered lashes. She thought him the most lovely sight she had ever seen. When Aegeus finally dropped his cup altogether, in an excess of good cheer, she was the first to run and pick it up.

The first to run, the first to slip in the puddle of spilled wine, the first to fall and the first to be caught up in Aegeus's two arms to keep her from falling.

He set her on her feet again and smiled, his eyes loose in his head from drinking and his lids heavy. Suddenly, all the bleariness left his eyes, like a sky blown clear of clouds, and the lids parted wider and wider still. 'I didn't, did I? I couldn't have.'

'What, my lord?' asked Aethra shyly.

'Never you mind, girl. Never you mind. I didn't . . . No, of course I didn't.' His mouth gave a small, anxious tug to one side, and very soon afterwards he said his goodnights and went to bed.

He slept heavily. His good mood was restored in the morning, and he climbed into his chariot, looped round with the end of his reins as happy as the crack at the end of a whip. At the last moment, he caught the eye of Aethra and whispered teasingly over the side of his chariot, 'I have left a present for you. At least, it's a present for your son, if you should ever—one day, you know—in the future—have a son. He'll find my sword and sandals under that rock—when he's man enough to lift it.'

Aethra cast bewildered eyes at the rock he pointed out—a boulder so huge that an oxen team could hardly have moved it. She shook her head, meaning that she did not understand his joke or why he should make fun of her. As he rode away, however, she still thought he was the most beautiful sight she had seen since she had seen a forest fire ravage the crown of a wooded hill and set all the wild birds flying.

As soon as Aegeus arrived home, he opened his arms to his wife and clasped her to his breast. 'Your armour's hard,' she complained, and pushed him away.

A few days later, she caught a fever and died.

Aegeus was too disappointed to be angry. He simply supposed that the Oracle at Delphi had made a mistake. Or perhaps the sorceress's magic had splashed off his hard breastplate.

More years arrived at the gates of Athens, one year after another. Years raced through the streets, through Aegeus's palace, and trampled over him like stampeding horses, leaving a sprinkling of grey in his hair, a network of lines on his face, a stoop.

Then Medea the sorceress arrived one day from Corinth, in a chariot drawn by two winged serpents. Aegeus thanked the gods for sending her. All she asked for was a place to shelter, out of the wind and sun. But Aegeus took her into the shelter of his palace, even into

7

the shelter of his bed. He married her. And there was more magic: she gave birth to a little boy—a prince for Athens . . . and called him *Medus*.

2

The Club and the Sword

'Where do you want me to put the basket of bread, mother?'

'Oh, in the middle of the table, I think, Theseus, where everyone can reach it. Though Hercules will eat it all, of course, as usual. When your cousin Hercules comes to dinner, nobody else gets much to eat.'

Theseus, who was seven years old, could not wait to see his cousin for the first time. People said he was the strongest man in the world. 'If I asked him, would he teach me how to wrestle, mother?'

The lady Aethra frowned. 'Fighting! Must you always be talking about fighting?'

'Does he have a sword, mother? Does Hercules have a sword?'

'No he doesn't. Just a big club.'

'How big, mother? As big as me?'

'Every bit as big. Now go and get washed. Do you mean Hercules to see you looking like the floor of the Augean stables?'

Before Theseus was washed, his cousin arrived—a man so laden with muscles that his body seemed to be coiled round with snakes. He wore for a cloak the skin of a lion he had fought and killed with his bare hands—not just the fur, but the head, too, with gaping jaws and staring eyes and creased, velvety cheeks. Hercules flung it over a stool where it happened to fall paws downwards, the head lolling towards the door.

'Come on! Come on! He's here! I heard him arrive!' cried Theseus to all the other children who lived in the house at Troezen. They came running from every direction, and all bundled through the door together.

They took one look at the lionskin—they took another—then they scattered. Screaming and shrieking, they ran for the stairs, they ran to the kitchen, they ran to their mothers and hid their faces and howled in terror that there was a lion in the dining hall. All except Theseus. He looked at the lionskin; he looked at his cousin; he looked at his mother, and then he backed towards the door—slowly, slowly. Between unmoving lips he whispered, 'Don't panic. Stay perfectly still.' After he had closed the door, his sandals could be heard pelting along the corridor.

Hercules laughed out loud, and all the goblets on the table trembled. But he stopped laughing when the noise of sandals came pelting back again. The door opened and in strode Theseus, dragging an axe almost as big as himself.

'Don't worry, mother. I'll deal with it! Shame on you, cousin, for letting a lion walk so close to my mother!' And he swung the axe with all his might.

Hercules thumped the table with his fist. 'By all the gods, boy! You've killed my cloak! And that stool will never walk again! Aethra, what a little Titan you've got there! Introduce me at once.'

So Theseus picked himself up off the floor (where the weight of the axe had thrown him) and shook hands with his cousin, the mighty Hercules. 'You have your mother's eyes, boy, but where do you get your fire from? Your father, maybe?'

Aethra dropped the plate she was holding. 'Haven't got a father, sir,' said Theseus cheerfully. 'Don't need one. I can look after mother well enough.'

'Theseus! How often must I tell you? Don't brag. I'm sorry, Hercules, but there's a streak of pride in the boy that the gods would frown on if they saw it. *You* speak to him. Tell him there's more to life than fighting and killing and having strong arms.'

Hercules plucked at his beard thoughtfully and slowly nodded. But his mind was somewhere else, and his eyes peered into Theseus's face. 'I've seen this face before. There's a certain noble gentleman in Athens with just the same face. When do you intend to tell the lad exactly who he is, Aunt Aethra?'

'When he's big enough and sensible enough,' said Aethra crossly, covering Theseus's two ears with her hands and hustling him out of the room.

Theseus nagged her every day, after that. 'Who am I, mother? What did Hercules mean? Do I have a father, after all?'

But Aethra only said, 'Soon enough. Soon enough you'll leave me. Soon enough there will be *real* lions lying in wait for you. Be content. There are more good things to be harvested from this world than what you can reap with a sword.'

In the days when Theseus was young, the world was young, too. Only a few ships were sprinkled on the world-encircled sea; only a few houses had grown up along its shores and river-banks. And what houses there were, were bare and barely higher than a man's head. Beds sprawled legless on the floor, and the grain and grapes rattled by in two-wheeled carts, pulled by small and pale-eared donkeys.

Men, too, were slight and lean, with narrow shoulders, and hips like hunting dogs—quick to look behind them, and narrow-eyed with looking out to sea.

Theseus, too, was lean as a boy. His ribs circled his chest like fingers, and his legs were as thin as grass. But as he grew up, the muscles plaited along his bones and his chest filled out like a ship's sail, and his neck grew from his chest like a thick-rooted tree. His hair shone like an otter's fur, but curled long and loose to his shoulder blades which were as smooth as the bronze plates of a prince's armour. And his eyes were such a turbulent blue that the superstitious peasants of Troezen said, 'There's the sea itself in those eyes. Poseidon the sea god must have fathered that boy!'

When Theseus was about seventeen, a sudden silence fell over Troezen—not the silence of people sleeping soundly in their beds, but the silence of people holding their breath in terror. They could almost hear the thump, thump of each other's hearts.

A monstrous man called Periphetes had come to the district—a man hunched over like a bear. As he walked, he left the splayed print of his left hand in the earth, and from his right hand he trailed a huge, bronze club. His head was the shape of a club; his nose was the shape of a club; even his brain was club-shaped, so much time did he spend thinking about clubbing.

Up and down the Corinth road Periphetes roamed. When he broke into a shambling run, he could keep pace with a horse and club the rider out of the saddle. He would smash down a roadside house and block the road with the rubble. Then when a cart was forced to stop, he would sneak up behind it and shatter the cart and squander the load and leave only the white-eyed horses to run off between their shafts. He clubbed cows and dogs; he clubbed fences and barns; he clubbed trees and wine vats. But chiefly he loved to club men and women who passed along 'his' road.

Word of Periphetes spread until nobody dared to travel from Corinth to Troezen, from Troezen to Corinth. 'Perhaps now he'll get bored and move on to a different place,' said the people of Troezen.

Periphetes did get bored when no one came along his road, when there was nobody to ambush and nobody to club. 'Betti moob on,' he thought with his club-shaped brain. 'Waygo nowbut? Corinff? Oober yonder-sider Troezen?'

Slowly, like a drip forming below his club-shaped brain, Periphetes formed an idea. 'Ohah! Clubben Troezen Igo! All de walk clubben, ander all de mennen, ander all de roof-underplaces, ander cartes ander animoos—ander prettiladies, ander babys, ander childer—yuck, Periphetes verihate childer.' And delighted with the idea of destroying Troezen brick by brick and bone by bone, the revolting Periphetes gambolled down the road towards the rooftops of the little village. As he ran, he left a groove as deep as a cart-rut, dragging his huge, bronze club.

The first Pittheus knew of the attack was when terrified peasants came hammering on his door. 'Let us in! Let us in! Periphetes is coming! Periphetes is destroying the town!'

They watched him from the roof, pounding the sheep-folds to pieces and pulverizing the cottages. The earth under the vines ran purple with their spilled juice, and the dry-stone walling tumbled in avalanches round the feet of Periphetes.

'Even if we bar the door, he'll club his way through

13

the walls!' whispered Pittheus. 'Aethra, hide yourself and hide the boy. Nothing will keep Periphetes out!'

But when Aethra went looking for Theseus to hide him from the club-man, she could not find him. Suddenly she heard her father calling the boy's name too, but urgently, distractedly: 'Theseus! Come back here! *Theseus!* What's he doing out there? What does he think he's doing?'

Theseus, his thumbs tucked into his cord belt, was scuffing his feet across the courtyard and out into the sunlight of the road. Past the gate he went, past the lemon tree, past the limes and into the yellow sunlight that dazzled on his tunic. Then he stopped, cocking his head on one side. He called out, 'Periphetes! Be off with you. You're not welcome here.'

'Greep! A verifool childer! A nearlidead bore! Comen closeup, bore! Periphetes grimpen ander grumpen yooz. Heep-eep-eep!' The club-man tossed the handle of his club from hand to hand and bared his teeth—curved as talons—at Theseus. Then he began to throw the club high into the air—higher each time—like a juggler. The sun flashed on the bronze. He caught it first with his right hand, then with his left, and now and then he caught it in both and smashed it down on the ground till there was a long shallow dent in the earth. 'Bed for bore. Make-I bed for veridead bore!' And he flung the club higher than ever into the air.

Theseus put down his head and charged. Like a bull he covered the ground, his arms doubled over his head to protect his skull from the jolt. As he rammed Periphetes, dust burst in clouds out of the giant's clothing and he let out a little, breathless grunt and sat down, hard. His massive club reached the zenith of its flight and began to come down again, still whirling. Theseus reached into the air and, with both hands, took hold of it. Once, twice, three times he brought it down on Periphetes's head.

It was not enough. The giant rocked from side to side, to and fro, but he did not fall over on to his back. In fact he drew up his knees as if he was about to get to his feet, and his two eyes struggled to focus on Theseus.

Theseus threw aside the club and seizing hold of a big boulder nearby, he raised it off the ground. As long as the span of his arms, it was, but he lifted it, clenching his teeth and bending his knees. And he half dropped, half threw it at Periphetes's head.

After that, Periphetes's head was no longer the shape of a club. Nor was his nose. Nor was his brain. And no thoughts of clubbing ever passed that way again. Periphetes was pretty much dead.

When he saw what he had done, and how easily he had done it, Theseus gave a great leap in the air and spread his hands towards heaven, as if to say, 'Did you see? Were you watching?' But there was no roll of thunder from the mountains of the gods, and behind him, the people of Troezen stood white-faced as if, all of a sudden, Theseus frightened them.

Then Pittheus began to stammer out congratulations and praise. He said he was very proud of his grandson, very proud indeed. The peasants and servants began to cheer and jig, whirling Theseus up in their dance. Only Aethra stood to one side, her face the colour of chalk. She called Theseus sharply to her side, took hold of his wrist, and led him away from the house, as if to scold him in private.

She led him back to the spot where he had lifted the boulder to throw at Periphetes, and she pointed at the ground. There was a shallow trench, and in it lay a sword and a pair of sandals.

'It is time to tell you. These were put here, under the rock, by your father. They're yours now, since you were man enough to uncover them . . . Don't interrupt. It is time for you to go and show yourself to your father. He'll be glad to see you—I'm sure of that—though he doesn't know yet that you exist. But you must be careful. Your father has more to give you than most fathers, and other people may grow to envy you.'

'You mean he's rich, mother? Or famous?'

'He is the king of the city-state of Athens, boy, and his name is Aegeus. Will you leave tomorrow? A boat will carry you all the way to Pyrrheus harbour: that's the safest way to go.'

'Then *I* shall go by road!' exclaimed Theseus, tipping back his head in that arrogant way that irritated his mother so much. '*I* never hankered after *safety*! My father has waited seventeen years to see me. He can wait a few days longer. Yes, I shall go to Athens by road, and maybe do a brave deed or two on the way that will make the gods stand up on Olympus to clap me.' And he flourished his father's sword so that it flashed in the sunlight and dazzled his mother and the others.

He kept the bronze club of Periphetes—a souvenir of his first victory.

3

On the Road to Athens

The air trembled in the heat of the sun. It looked as if the countryside ahead was melting. The trees wavered in the shimmering haze, and watery mirages puddled and evaporated on the roadway.

Theseus, his long hair hanging dark with sweat between his shoulder blades, was watching the horizon wrinkle like damp paper when, all of a sudden, he saw an extraordinary sight. Two huge trees were not just wavering in the heat haze—they were bending down, like two men bowing to each other, bowing from the waist. Their tips almost touched, then the trees went on bending and bending until they were hooped right over—arched like a greyhound's back. Then they righted themselves with a noise of lashing branches and a shriek that stopped Theseus in his tracks. Two black shapes rocketed across the sky in opposite directions, as though the trees had tossed their hats in the air.

'So far from home, and the trees themselves have heard tell of my fight with Periphetes! Are they really bowing down to me? Cheering me?' The sight so amazed him that he did not notice the man who stepped out on

17

to the road ahead of him. Theseus walked straight into him. 'Sorry,' said Theseus irritably.

Then two hands took hold of his shoulders and lifted him up and threw him—ooff—across a shoulder, as if he were a sack of sand. 'Where's your permit, stringbean? Where's your authorization to walk along my road?'

'Who are you? What permit? Whose road? Put me down, I demand it!'

'Oh-ho! Demand away, little spring onion. In the meantime, the trees are waiting.'

'Take care, sir! I am Theseus, prince of Athens, who took the bronze club of Periphetes and beat him with it! Do you want to suffer the same fate?'

'Who? Never heard of him. Never heard of you. But I'll warrant you've heard of me, little beetroot. I'm the Tree-Bender of the Isthmus!'

They reached a clearing among tall cypress trees. A rope hung down from the tallest tree on either side of the glade. Setting Theseus down beside a sapling, he buckled his huge belt round both Theseus and the sapling, to hold him fast. Then he hauled on one of the ropes, his muscles bulging like the crust of a plaited loaf. The tree wagged, then began to bend, until its top was pulled right down into the clearing. Trapping the topmost branches under his huge heel, the Tree-Bender began to haul on the other rope, until the tree on the other side of the glade had also bent itself in two. He cracked the two rope-ends in Theseus's face.

'Now! This end goes round your *left* ankle, and this end goes round your *right*. Then when I let go—*schrrquwczzz*—two one-legged men and both of them called Theseus! One in the eastern provinces and one in the west. Won't you just split your sides laughing, eh, little cabbage! And what a deal of squelching blood

18

there'll be. I like blood and gore, I do. Nobody likes it more than me.'

When both trees were fully bent, the Tree-Bender held them down with his two huge heels while he unfastened his belt and freed Theseus—and held him upside down by his feet.

Theseus's head dangled down. He twisted and writhed, but the Tree-Bender held him fast with one elbow, while knotting one rope-end round Theseus's left ankle. The king's sword and the bronze club of Periphetes lay out of reach beside the sapling . . .

There were coils of slack rope heaped to either side. Theseus picked up a loop in both hands then, squirming round, sank his teeth into the giant's leg. It was no more than a gnat sting to the Tree-Bender, but he lifted his toes just for a moment. Theseus twisted the other way, bit the other ankle. The giant just laughed at his struggling—but he did lift his toes for a moment with the pain. It was long enough for Theseus to slip a loop of rope round that foot, too. The next moment, like an acrobat, Theseus swung himself between the giant's legs, reached up and caught hold of the Tree-Bender's belt, then launched kicks in every direction, until the Tree-Bender was forced to let go.

Irritably, the giant dropped Theseus on his head and raised one foot to stamp on him . . . The bent pine tree escaped from under his heel and sprang upright. The Tree-Bender flew into the air. There was hardly time for screaming before the left-hand tree straightened up and— *schrrquwczzz*—the Tree-Bender left in two directions at once.

When Theseus saw what he had done and how easily he had done it, he gave a great leap in the air and spread his hands towards heaven as if to say, 'Did you see? Were you watching?' But there was no roll of thunder from the mountains, no roar from the sea.

19

* * *

Just beyond the Isthmus, Theseus came to a village where the houses were all built on stilts. He was hungry, and would have asked for a meal, but no one was out working in the fields, no one at all. 'Hey! Hello there! Anybody! Where are you all?' And he rapped on the stilt of a house. A rope snaked past his face.

'Quick, boy! Climb up, you reckless fool! Don't you know the boar's about?'

'What bore?' said Theseus, disdaining to climb up the rope.

The woman of the house looked down at him from the threshold of the hut. 'The Crommyonian Boar, of course!'

'The what?'

'The Crommyonian Boar.'

'A big bore to warrant such a long name,' said Theseus.

'Oh, vast! Enormous! Huge! It's driven us out of our own fields and killed more than a dozen men who went to hunt it! Before we built our houses on stilts its tusks came smashing through the walls—right in the middle of supper!'

'Oh, *that* kind of a boar,' said Theseus, grinning. 'A little wild pig, you mean.'

The woman's eyes shifted from Theseus's face and across his shoulder. The platform on which her hut rested began to tremble. So did the woman. 'Look out! *Look out!* It's the Crommyonian bo—'

The name was so long that by the time she had said it, there was no time left for climbing the rope. Theseus turned and saw a boar as big as a rhinoceros, its tusks crossed over its nose like two great sabres, and thundering towards him so fast that its legs were a blur of movement in a blur of dust.

Theseus put two hands to the rope, jumped and tucked his knees up to his chin. The Crommyonian Boar trampled by beneath him, and the bristles of its back brushed his shins. It collided with one of the stilts of the platform, and brought the hut tumbling down on its head with a noise of splintering wood. The woman of the house, a baby clutched in her arms, ran shrieking towards the sea. The Crommyonian Boar got up and shook itself: its thick, short legs bowed outwards under the massive weight of its furious body. It lowered its head to charge.

Theseus too picked himself up from among the wreckage of the hut and snatched up the bronze club he had taken from Periphetes. As the boar came on, he lifted the club two-handed over his shoulder. As the crossed tusks rattled in his face, he swung the club—and he knocked the Crommyonian Boar—like a batsman striking a ball. Hoof-over-horn the Crommyonian Boar cartwheeled through the air and landed insensible in a patch of sea-pinks. It was only a matter then of taking hold of the monstrous white tusks and snapping the beast's neck. Painlessly he delivered the big pig into the safe-keeping of the goddess Artemis, who tends the spirits of all dead boars.

When he saw what he had done and how easily he had done it, Theseus gave a great leap in the air and spread his hands towards heaven as if to say, 'Did you see? Were you watching?' But there was no roll of thunder from the hills, no roar from the sea—only the timid clapping of the Crommyonian villagers as they lowered themselves down from their huts-on-stilts and stood about, wide-eyed.

Beyond the village, the path grew narrow—a gouge cut in

the side of a steep cliff, with beetling rocks rising to the left and a precipice falling into the sea on the right. Theseus paused to admire the view. A sharp wind was piling up waves against the rocks below. But the pathway ahead showed up like a white, zigzag scar on the face of the cliff. Screwing up his eyes, Theseus caught sight of another traveller ahead of him on the path. After two days of walking, he hankered after some company, and quickened his steps to catch up with the man.

He was only a little out of hailing distance when the man on the road ahead stopped. His way was barred by a human creature as round as a boulder.

Theseus had to pick his way carefully for fear of falling over the cliff-edge. He could not hear what words passed between the two, but the traveller all at once leaned down as if to fasten the other's shoe. In one quick and practised movement, the fat ambusher seized hold of him, belt and collar, and flung the unwary traveller over the brink of the cliff!

The scream was carried away by the gulls. But one thing heard it. Down in the sea, a ring of white foam spread where the traveller had plunged headlong into the water. Alongside it, another ring formed, as though a rock was drying out as the tide ebbed. It was round and hard like a rock as it rose out of the water. But a rock does not have a head at one end and stumpy cylindrical legs to either side. A great grey turtle reared up out of the surf, bigger than a rowing boat, bigger than a cow, bigger even than the Crommyonian Boar.

It chewed at the water, its gaping square head like a box, opening and closing. It devoured the traveller and cast a pebbly glance up the cliff face, as though it was accustomed to the treat.

The loose chalk trickled from under Theseus's sandals and over the precipice. He picked his way very carefully along the path to the place where the fat man sat barring the way.

'You! Small fry!'

'Who? Me?'

'Where do you think you're going?'

'To Athens, sir,' said Theseus courteously, although the hairs on his neck were beginning to stir, as the hackles rise on an angry dog.

'Not without paying the toll. I'm Sciron—the Guardian of the Highway.'

'Not much of a highway,' said Theseus, kicking some chalky scree into the sea below.

'Well, it's *high*, isn't it? And it's the *way* from where you've been to where you're going. So. Are you going to pay the toll or go back where you came from?' Sciron was a one-eyed man with shoulders so wide, a back so short and a head so flat and neckless that he was the same shape as the boulders round about him.

'What is the toll?' asked Theseus.

'You must tie my sandals for me. I'm too fat to reach my feet.'

So Theseus laid down his bronze club and twisted his sword so that its blade was out of the way. And he stooped down in front of Sciron and took hold of the loose sandal straps.

With fingers as quick as a conjuror, he bound the ankles together with three overhand knots, then, with interlocking hands, he made a stirrup for the fat man's foot and pitched him, heels-over-head off his boulder and over the edge of the cliff.

The great grey turtle had not eaten so well for a long time.

When Theseus saw what he had done and how easily he had done it, he gave a great leap in the air and spread his hands towards heaven, as if to say, 'Did you see?

Were you watching?' But there was no roll of thunder from the mountains, no roar from the sea—only the champing of the great grey turtle in the sea below.

Athens was already in sight when Theseus passed a troop of soldiers on the road. He was still wearing his sword down behind his knees, and his club was inside his long cloak. The soldiers, their arms round each other's necks, called out, 'What's a pretty girl like you doing out here on your own?'

'By the gods, you're a buxom wench and no mistake!'

'Big enough for two husbands, eh!'

Theseus twisted his sword back on to his hip and spread his cloak so that they could see his bronze club; they stumbled off with a howl of laughter, laughing at their own mistake as much as at Theseus. He did not trouble to pick a fight with them. But, watching them go, he did see that it was not the way of Athenian men to wear their hair loose down their backs. He thought, I must make myself presentable. I can't have my father thinking he has a daughter instead of a son!

So he knocked at the first house he came to, a fine, expensive villa cloaked in vines and with horses grazing outside. The owner was most hospitable: 'Come in! Come in, young lady! Oh dear, I *am* sorry—what a foolish mistake! Can I offer you a bed for the night, young sir?'

The man, whose name was Corydallus, took Theseus to a clean, comfortable room, brought him a basin of water and several candles, as it was getting dark. When Theseus asked his advice as to how to wear his hair, Corydallus told him, 'You must plait your hair behind and crop it really short in front. That way your opponent in battle won't be able to catch hold of your forelock

24

while he cuts your throat! Here are the shears, young friend. When you've done, I'll show you to your bed. But you'll excuse me now. You're not the first traveller to stop at my house this evening.'

Theseus set about plaiting his long hair and then cutting away the golden curls that had coiled across his forehead for fully fifteen years. As the curls dropped down, it was like seeing his childhood fall to the floor, or the petals of a rose drop when the hard hip ripens. He paused in his snipping to pick up a handful of hair.

As he stooped down, his ear came close to the wall. His sharp hearing picked up the sound—there was no mistaking it—of a man choking. He crossed quickly to the window, stepped through it into the garden, and moved along the wall to the window of the next room.

There, Corydallus was putting two young men to bed—for ever. One was tall, the other short. The beds he gave them were of a standard length, but it was the rule of this gruesome house that every visitor must fit his bed exactly. So, when the one was too long for his mattress, Corydallus lopped off his head. And now he was stretching the little man to fit his bed. Theseus turned away and shut his eyes.

He wondered whether to slip away then and there, and tell his father, when he reached Athens, to send soldiers to arrest Corydallus. But then he drew his sword and, by the light of the moon, looked at his reflection in its blade. The face looking back at him was an angry, unfamiliar, and fierce face, with no golden curls across the forehead to make it gentle. He climbed back through the window of his room and waited for Corydallus to show him to his bed.

'This way, this way!' said Corydallus cheerfully, bowing a little with every word. He showed Theseus to the selfsame bedroom: there was no sign of the two young men he had murdered. 'You're a tall gentleman, aren't you, sir? I fear you may find my humble bed a little uncomfortable.'

'Bed? What's a bed?' said Theseus, smiling wide-eyed at Corydallus. When he was shown the two beds in the room, he shook his head in bafflement. 'Yes, but what do you *do* with them?'

Corydallus scratched his head. 'Zeus, what a peasant you are, boy. I suppose you sleep in the hay at home. Town folk sleep on *beds.*'

'Sleep? What's sleep?' said Theseus, grinning excitedly.

Corydallus began to be vexed. '*Sleep*. You know, zzz zzzzz!' And he snored loudly and shut his eyes and rested his head against his hands.

When he opened his eyes again, Theseus was still gawping at him, and seemed to be trying to imitate a snore. 'Oink-oink?' he said. 'Like a pig?'

'Well! I'll go to the foot of Olympus, I never met such a stupid young bumpkin! Everyone *sleeps*. Look—like this.' And Corydallus lay down on the nearest bed.

'Looks to me as if you're a little short for that bed,' said Theseus and, taking hold of both ends of Corydallus—hair and feet—he stretched him until he was a *much* taller man. 'Oh dear. I seem to have over-stretched you, sir. Now you're too long for the bed. No matter. I have a sword here to put that to rights . . . '

Next day, Theseus shut the door of the house behind him and walked the last mile into Athens. His hair was plaited and the plait hung down to the base of his shoulder blades. But the front was cut short to show that he was a fighting man and an Athenian.

4

An Assassination Attempt

In the morning sunlight, a hundred tiny emerald lizards were basking on the white walls of the king's long, low palace. A little boy was throwing stones at them, trying to squash them or knock them off one by one. They scurried and scattered, but Medus was a very poor shot.

'Can you direct me to the king?' asked Theseus. He had already asked the servants, but they were too busy to answer, rushing to and fro with panniers and baskets, preparing for a feast.

The little boy said, 'Do you really expect me to speak to you? Do you know who I am? I'm the Prince of Athens! I'm Prince Medus!'

Theseus smiled tolerantly. 'So. I have a brother, and I didn't even know.'

'What did you call me? I'll have you torn to pieces between four chariots. You're not my brother. Haven't got a brother. Go away or I'll tell mother.'

Theseus was tempted to thrash the boy soundly, but instead he only patted Medus on the head. 'And just who is your mother, child?'

27

Just then, Medea came to the door to call her son. At the sight of Theseus she dropped the bowl she was holding, and black olives rolled about her feet. Medus let fly with his fists, and pummelled Theseus in the thigh. 'Look what you've done! Mother! Mother! He says he's my brother. Have him hung, mother! Have him fed to the catfish in tiny little pieces!'

'A dear child,' said Theseus politely to Medea.

'Medus! Stop that. Shake hands with your brother. My dear stepson. I knew at once who you must be. You're the very image of your father—a little taller, perhaps, and your eyes are bluer, but I can see for myself who you are . . . Medus, don't eat those, there's a good boy.'

The little boy was squatting on his haunches, eating the spilled olives off the ground, one by one, spitting the stones at Theseus, and muttering with his mouth full, 'Not my brother. Haven't got a brother.'

But Medea made Theseus as welcome as if he were her own son. She took him indoors and gave him breakfast, then showed him all the rooms of the palace (except for the king's). Theseus was too well-mannered to show his impatience, but his eyes were all about him as he went, hoping to catch a glimpse of his father.

Suddenly, Medea rested one hand on Theseus's arm as if an idea had struck her. 'Oh, such a joke! It would be such a joke! Will you do something for me, Theseus?'

'Madam, anything.'

'Then don't let's tell Aegeus who you are. Let's see if he can recognize you for himself! Come to the feast tonight as a stranger—and see if he can spot his own likeness in you. I'll make him pay a forfeit to you of a hundred golden pieces if he can't! Oh say you'll do it— for the sport of it.'

28

'Madam, I've waited seventeen years to meet my father. I can be patient until tonight, of course I can!'

As he left, intending to spend the day exploring the city and its sights, Medus tripped him up in the doorway, and ran grizzling to his mother when Theseus slapped him. 'Get rid of him, mother! Don't like him. Got more hair than me!'

His mother spread her skirts and wrapped them round Medus and hugged him close. 'If only that were all, my darling boy. Don't you understand? He was born before you were. That makes *him* the true heir to Athens. He'll disinherit you, boy. And I shall have to watch another woman's son take the throne ahead of you . . . Come with me, Medus—*and stop grizzling!*'

King Aegeus was kept busy all day with preparations for the feast. Whenever he caught sight of his wife, he saw her anxiously gnawing her lip. When at last they sat down alongside each other, at the head of the table, he leaned on the arm of his chair and asked, 'Is something troubling you, my dear?'

She too leaned on the arm of her chair and her head bent close to his. 'Spies, my dear.'

'Pies?'

'*Spies*, my dear. *Spies*. Athens is full of them, of course, but I never thought your enemies would dare to send a spy into the palace itself, in broad daylight. The gall! The treachery!'

Aegeus started up out of his chair. 'Where? Who is it? Who told you, Medea?'

Medea laid her finger to her lips. 'No need to alarm your guests. I have my arts, haven't I? I can see into a man's heart. I can see when he's plotting assassination.'

'Assassination!?' spluttered Aegeus.

'And I know how to stop a man's heart beating for ever,' said Medea. 'You see the youth there with blond hair cut like an Athenian fighting man—the one with the blue eyes. I've heard him speak, and he's no Athenian. He's a boy from the country, and he's here in the pay of that Cretan villain, Minos. And he's wearing a sword under that cloak.'

It crossed the king's mind that most of his guests were wearing swords and that many came from outside Athens. But his wife had magic powers and, after all, why should she lie to him? When you are married to a sorceress, it is all too easy to say, 'What must I do now, my dear?'

'It is all in hand,' said Medea. 'I have told the servant to poison the assassin's wine. Look. The beaker has just been set down beside his hand. Watch him drink and die.'

Theseus caught Medea's eye and winked. He fingered the metal of the wine beaker set down beside him. His mother, Aethra, had told him to avoid strong wine, gambling, and strange women. But his mother was in Troezen, wasn't she? He had a good mind to drink it down in one swig and call for more. He wanted his father to see him for the grown man he was. He picked up the beaker.

But when he raised it to his lips, the reflection of his own face so startled him that he hesitated and sat staring into the wine at his newly shorn forehead and curl-less cheeks. Then his father's voice addressed him.

'Young man. Yes, you. Why don't you make yourself useful and carve meat for us all?'

Medea ground her teeth. 'What are you doing? He was just about to drink!' she hissed.

'I like to see the man I'm killing,' whispered her

husband smugly. 'Look at the size of him, and the muscles on his arm. I'm glad my enemies didn't insult me by sending some weakling to assassinate me. What is he waiting for? Why doesn't he carve?'

Theseus was in fact gazing at the roast lamb that stood on the table in front of him. He had never in his life carved a joint of meat. He had never even watched with interest his mother or grandfather carve at table. Did his father already recognize him that he drew special attention to him? Did he want Theseus to make a fool of himself in front of all these people because he could not carve? Besides, he had no dagger. What should he use for a carving knife? Nervousness made him thirsty. A sip of wine and then he would make an attempt on the meat. No, his father might think he needed the wine to steady his nerves. For the second time, Theseus put down his cup.

A sudden idea came to him. If he could not carve well, at least he would carve with panache. And, drawing his sword, he flourished it dramatically, meaning to chop the roast lamb into a hundred pieces . . .

'At my own table he draws his sword to kill me!' stormed Aegeus, knocking over his chair as he leapt up. 'Guards! Cut him down! Show this assassin how the court of Athens rewards treachery!' Beside the king, his queen clutched her son to her bosom as if to protect him from the flying blades. But there was a smug smile on her lips, and little Medus was grinning. He stuck out his tongue at Theseus who was gaping in amazement at Queen Medea. Twenty armed soldiers closed in for the kill.

Theseus shook himself. 'Well, if that's the way of it!' he cried, and leapt on to the table, his sword raised in front of his chest to deflect the first blows.

'WAIT! WAIT! WAIT!'

King Aegeus too had leapt on to the table. He held both hands in the air and his face was blue with the exertion of shouting. 'He's got my sword. *He's got my sword! And my sandals, too!'*

'Thief! Thief!' bawled the soldiers, and they began to rain blows on Theseus's parrying sword.

'No! No! STOP!' bellowed the king, tearing his hair and lunging in among the clashing blades at great danger to his life. 'He's no thief! I *gave* the sword and sandals to him before he was ever born. Stranger! No one could have lifted that rock except one boy—and he with the help of the immortal gods. If you are that boy, then you are the one the Oracle promised! You are Theseus! *You are my son!'*

The feast broke up in disorder. In all the jostling and pushing, Theseus's beaker was spilled, and raised large, blistering burns on the surface of the table. Medea and Medus tried to creep away in the confusion, but Aegeus glimpsed them climbing through the window, and sent his guards to fetch them back. 'Soon enough you may go!' he told them. 'Soon enough you may take the clothes you are wearing and a chariot from the stables and leave Athens for ever. You are banished, Medea, and your spoiled brat is disinherited. This is my real heir, and his mother shall be Queen of Athens. Theseus, put my mind at rest this instant. Is your mother's name Aethra of Troezen? Yes? I knew it! Somewhere sewn into the seams of my heart I've carried the thought of your mother with me all along. Come down, son. I have a kingdom to give you. But first you shall finish carving the meat so that everyone here can feast in your honour!'

So Medea and Medus left the city-state of Athens in a squeaking chariot and a cloud of dust, like shame, that hung over them all the way to the horizon. Watching them go, King Aegeus thought, This is why the Oracle said my son would bring me grief.

32

Theseus was declared Prince of Athens, and wore round his shorn forelocks a plaited band of white gold that shone almost as brightly as his eyes. Aethra was brought from Troezen to be Aegeus's queen, and after that the king began to doubt the wisdom of the Delphic Oracle. There was little grief in having Theseus for a son. In fact, if it were not for the matter of Minos, King of Crete, Aegeus would have been the happiest man alive.

5

The Bull's Child

In the days when Theseus was Prince of Athens on the shores of the sea, Poseidon the Earth-Shaker, the Earthquake-Maker, the sea god himself ruled the oceans. And in the paddock ocean which stretched from the shores of Hellas to the island of Crete, he grazed his great blue bull.

Wherever Poseidon's bull roamed, men who looked out to sea, or sailors who gazed over their ship's rails on a stormy day, said that they could see the arch of its monumental neck and hear it bellowing out a challenge to the fishes of the deep. Its legs were the bent pillars of waterspouts, and its feet were splayed spray, and its head had a certain terrible beauty, too.

There was one person who looked out to sea more often than most. Forced by her marriage to the king of Crete to live out her life on the island, the lonely Queen Pasiphae often stood on the beaches and watched for Poseidon's bull. She made garlands to hang around its horns, and it learned to come looking for the haystacks of field flowers she set out on the shore. And as the bull ate, Pasiphae would stand hem-deep in the lapping water, and stroke her hand over its blue neck.

At last it grew so tame that she was able to straddle its back and ride the length of the long, deserted beaches. As she did so, she whispered into its flickering ears until it strode into the sea and tumbled her in the thrill of the surf. Sometimes it came to her with the ropes and spars of wrecked ships trailing from its horns, and then she would praise its strength and ask how many men it had drowned, and the bull would beat out the reply with its pacing hoof. In short, Pasiphae loved the beast with a love she had never shown to the king of Crete. And when a child was born to Queen Pasiphae, it bore no likeness to the king.

It had the chest and arms of a man, with the whitest of white skin and muscles as huge as the ruts of a cart-track. But its head and hips and hooves were those of a bull calf, and it grew to the size of a man in one year. Full grown, it stood horn and dewlap taller than the king himself, and its shoulders were hunched like the keel of a rowing boat. It crunched and ate the servants who brought it food.

When King Minos saw his wife's 'son' he knew well enough what had happened. He had a tower built as a prison for Pasiphae, and he had a pen made, too, for her bull-child. He tried to keep its birth a secret, but rumour spread from end to end of Crete that the queen's monster was chained up beneath the palace, and at night people could hear it bellowing.

Summoning to Crete the inventor-genius Daedalus, King Minos said, 'Build me a new palace—a palace worthy of a king who commands the sea-lanes of the world. I want a building so tall that by standing on the roof I can see a mile out to sea. And I want a cellar—a big cellar—bigger than the palace, and twisting like a maze. It doesn't need windows or steps or ladders or exits—just a grating here and there where meat can be pushed through—oh, and a trapdoor large enough to drop a man through. Its corridors must wind and weave so much that someone could wander for a year and never find his bearings. And at the heart of the cellar I want a cell with a manger and a mattress and a cake of salt . . . They call it the Minotaur, Daedalus, isn't that right?'

'I don't know what you mean, sir,' said the inventor nervously.

'I know what people are saying, man. They call it the Minotaur—the beast of Minos. But it's no son of mine. I never want to lay eyes on it again. I'll keep it, even so. I'll use it to make myself the terror of the empire. When people on the mainland talk about Crete, they'll lower their voices and say, ''That's where the Minotaur lives in the king's cellar and eats human flesh!'' Do it, Daedalus—and build quickly. The beast gets stronger every week. It may break free any day . . . '

So Daedalus went back to his room and worked night and day to draw up plans for the new palace and its maze of cellars. His young son woke up in the early hours, and asked questions, never-ending questions about the plans his father was drawing. But Daedalus would not answer. He only said, 'Be a good boy, Icarus, and go back to bed, or the Minotaur may come and eat you up.' At that moment, a bellow rang through the silent palace, and Daedalus and the little boy both shuddered.

When the great blue bull came looking for Pasiphae and could not find her; when there were no more heaps of drying flowers on the shore nor garlands for his horns, the beast grew angry and raged up and down the ocean-world, destroying ships, lighthouses, and breakwaters, undermining cliffs and shivering coral reefs into clouds of blood-red sand. Last of all, it vented its fury on the sea-wall at Pyrrheus—the harbour below Athens where Aegeus and the Athenian merchants moored their vessels.

The wall was high and curved, and the bull's horns glanced off its slabs of white marble until sparks flew up and were mistaken, out at sea, for lightning. The owners of the ships in harbour ran to the waterfront, thinking to make fast the ropes, or off-load their cargoes. But when they saw the bulging blue skull of the bull, and the scimitar slash of its horns rearing up over the sea-wall, they fled in terror, praying out loud to Poseidon. 'O mighty Earth-Shaker and Earthquake-Maker and Shifter-of-the-seas! Your sacred bull is smashing the world to atomies! Save us! Save us from the bull!'

Close by, at the temple of Athena, Theseus happened to arrive, to make his daily sacrifice to the goddess of Athens. But all the sacrificial birds were sold; there was not a stick of incense to be had, and all the white meal in the city was scattered on the altar of Poseidon.

'What nonsense is this?' demanded the Prince of Athens and, strolling down to the harbour at Pyrrheus, he walked the length of the sea-wall, pausing now and then as the great blue bull charged and shook it to its foundations.

A gaping cleft had been riven in the towering wall, and the sea spewed through with every successive wave. Theseus straddled the gap and taunted the bull: 'You blown dandelion! You puff-ball! You melting snowball! Is that the best you can do? Fighting walls is about your mark. It would be different if you had to fight an opponent with brains!'

Poseidon's bull pawed the sea into a turmoil of seething currents and raised a bellow which holed the clouds on its way to Olympus. Poseidon the Sea-Shifter cocked an ear to listen. Looking down from a terrace of the holy mountain, he

37

was amused to see his great blue bull charge on the harbour. Athena's city will be a sorry sight by the time my pet has trampled through its streets, he thought, laughing.

On came the bull, its breastbone raising a chevron wave that spilled over the wall and almost dislodged Theseus from his perch. Directly at Theseus the bull charged, the thick bone of its forehead showing yellow through its smooth, blue hide. It fixed its aim on the arrogant mortal straddling the crack in the wall, and it hurled itself at him.

High into the air Theseus flung himself, as if he were leaping the new moon and not just the crescent of huge, goring horns. The bull's head went through the crack in the wall. So did its throat. But the thick, hurtling body wedged in the gap.

It took only the weight of Theseus landing on the tossing horns to snap the bull's short neck. Outside the sea-wall, its gross body bobbed harmlessly on the lessening waves: dead.

When Theseus saw what he had done and how easily he had done it, he gave a great leap in the air and spread his hands towards heaven, as if to say, 'Did you see? Were you watching?' But no roll of thunder came from the mountains, only a groan from the sea and a jaundice-yellowing of the sky over Athens and a kind of smell on the wind.

With the help of cheering Athenians, who showered him with flowers and kisses, Theseus hauled the dead bull through the streets of Athens to the Temple of Athena. 'This morning there were no sacrifices on sale when I came to worship the goddess Athena: they had all been spent on the altar of Poseidon,' declared the prince, one foot raised on the lolling head of the dead animal. 'But now I have a gift for the grey-eyed Athena more fitting than a scrawny pigeon or a sickly whiff of incense. Here on the altar of Pallas Athene I spill the blood of a worthy sacrifice!' And he drew his sword across the bull's throat. Ice-flecked, purple blood stained the marble everlastingly.

The jaundice yellow remained in the sky all that month, and the smell in the wind, too. It was an acrid smell, as though the doors of a heavenly cattle shed had been left ajar. Then the same sickly colour crept into the faces of the palace servants, and the king's guard. Men and women began to fall down in the streets, and the sound of children crying could be heard all night long. There was sickness within the walls of Athens.

There was plague.

6

Flying in the Face of the Gods

There were no longer emerald green lizards basking on the walls of the royal palace. They had all been frightened into the eaves and crevices by the shouting mob hurling rocks. 'It's Theseus's fault! Theseus brought it on us! Theseus killed Poseidon's bull!' yelled the mob, and tore up the laurel bushes in the garden.

'Take no notice,' said King Aegeus to his son, inside the palace, as the guards boarded up the last windows and the rooms were plunged into darkness. But the shutters did not keep out the angry chanting: *'Theseus brought the plague! Theseus brought the plague! Theseus brought down Poseidon's curse!'*

'Perhaps they're right,' said Theseus, though his nostrils flared and his lip curled with disgust. Only a month ago the same mob had been cheering him for breaking the bull's neck.

'There's only one way to find out, son. I must ask the Oracle Xenoclea why the gods have poured down this plague on us. She may even know what we must do to be rid of it.'

'I'll go, then. I'll go to Delphi,' said Theseus, pacing up and down the dark room.

'No. You must stay here with your mother. She's so ill, and if it really is the plague, she'll want you here with her. But take care not to catch it yourself, son. It may be that the gods will demand my life in exchange for their forgiveness. Athens must not be left without a ruler.'

Theseus opened his mouth to argue, but what could he say? Could even he gainsay the gods? He sat down in the corner of the room and folded his arms over his bowed head to blot out the sound of the chanting.

So King Aegeus travelled once more to the temple-cave at Delphi with its floor hollowed by a million feet, the yellow, retchy smoke and the befuddled maiden balanced on her pedestal of bronze, seeing visions.

'O sacred Oracle, who sees the past and the future as the view from a window, my poor city Athens is riddled with plague. Why? What have my people done wrong?'

At first, it seemed that the Oracle would not speak. Her closed eyes stared through Aegeus, and her jaw sagged and her hair hung in tangles to the floor. Were the gods too angry even to show him a sign? When the voice came, it sounded all the more dreadful for its toneless, pitiless calm:

'You know full well why Athens is being punished. Your son, Theseus, killed Poseidon's blue bull. Did he expect to go scot-free? The bull has a child. The gods decree that the bull's calf must be fed.'

'The bull's calf? Where is it? I'll give it all the plains round Athens to graze on, and have a host of maidens weave garlands for its neck!'

'Silence, Aegeus. Even you and your Athenians have heard tell of the bull's calf. It is called the Minotaur

41

and it lives on Crete where King Minos keeps it locked in the Labyrinth beneath his palace and feeds it on the flesh of maidens and men. Send seven young men and seven young women to Crete to feed the Minotaur, and Poseidon will lift his curse off the city of Athens. Such a little fine. Is the god of the sea not generous?' The slurred voice did not rise or fall one note. But as Aegeus turned to go, it pursued him into the daylight. 'Did I not warn you, Aegeus, that a son would bring you sorrow?'

'But have I not dealt fairly with you, man?' said King Minos. 'Have I not honoured our contract, to the letter?'

'Yes, yes. Of course. To the letter, my lord,' mumbled Daedalus. 'It's just that my conscience . . . My conscience, lord king.'

'Have I not supplied you with the finest materials, the best workmen? Have I not paid you in full and better?'

'Your majesty has been generous in everything. It's just that my conscience . . . ' The architect of the Labyrinth saw the patterns of the carpet on which he knelt squirm and writhe, as the monsters did in his nightmares, his many nightmares. Words deserted him. How was it to be said, without sounding critical of the king? And who criticizes a murderous king and lives? How was Daedalus to say that he hated the very thought of what he had done for King Minos. In designing and building the basement maze beneath the palace, he had become a party to the daily cruelty, the daily butchery, the daily waking nightmare. Daedalus had built the Labyrinth and now boys the same age as his own son were wandering its passageways. In his dreams he took their place, feeling his way through the dark, waiting for the moment when he turned a corner and came face to face with the Minotaur . . .

'Have I not housed you in comfort?' the king persisted. 'Has my hospitality somehow fallen short while you have been staying here as my guest? Do tell me, and I will make amends.' There was a sneer in his voice, a lack of interest in the queasiness of his hired man.

Daedalus confessed that he and his boy had lived in perfect luxury since arriving on Crete—a luxury unheard of in their home town of far-away Athens. He did not dare confess to the feeling that the tower-top room of theirs, with its gilded door and the soldiers posted outside, put him in mind of a prison. 'It's my conscience,' he said again lamely. 'It's just my conscience . . . '

'You do not like my Minotaur? If you had your way, you would starve it to death, I suppose. Did you never ask yourself, before you began work, what you were designing and to what purpose it might be put? No. No. I see you did not. The challenge of the project appealed to your inventor's brain. The originality of the assignment appealed to your architect's genius. Very well. You may go. I shall have your baggage packed for you. Go on! You are free to go. Let it never be said that Minos dealt unfairly with his hirelings.'

Hurriedly, barely able to believe his luck, Daedalus scrabbled to his feet; the carpet had left the imprint of its woollen pile on his knees. 'Your majesty is gracious—as ever—generous past measure! Thank you! Oh, thank you!' He turned for the door.

'Just one thing, Daedalus . . . '

'Yes, my lord?'

'I'm afraid I must insist that your son Icarus stays. My beast will be hungry again tomorrow. Your boy will serve to feed it.'

43

The inventor uttered a strangled cry and dropped all his parchment plans on the floor. He went down on his knees to gather them up, and stayed there, begging to be allowed to stay. 'You won't hear another word—not a word! Not Icarus! Not my boy! He's my whole life!'

King Minos smiled through his beard and nodded magnanimously. 'I am so glad I have managed to persuade you. Your lives will not be unpleasant here. I shall find many tasks for you that make use of your genius. It's just that you know the secret, you see. The solution to the puzzle. The answer to the conundrum. The map of the Labyrinth is locked within your brain, Daedalus. So you see I must keep you close at hand. You understand that, I'm sure. The secret of the map must be kept close at hand.'

Daedalus ran from the throne room. He ran down corridors he had designed himself and made beautiful with leaping lapis dolphins and scrolled sea patterns. The pictures were loathsome to him now; the dolphins seemed to leer and sneer at him, mocking his stupidity, saying, *Did you really expect the king to let you go? Ever? The map of the Labyrinth is in your brain*. Daedalus knew it all too well, for surely now, as he clawed at his hair and dragged his wrist across his drizzling eyes and nose, he could feel his very own monster rampaging and bellowing around the labyrinth of his brain: ugly, desperate, raging, detestable. Trapped.

As he reached the grid in the floor through which the Minotaur's food was dropped, he stumbled over his son, crouched in the shadows, peering down into the passages of the Labyrinth. 'Icarus, get up! Come away. How can you sit there hour after hour watching for that *monster*?'

Icarus protested at being dragged away from the grid. 'But I like to see it crunch on the bones, father! I like the way it picks them clean then crunches on them.'

Daedalus cast a despairing look at his son. 'There's no time to waste,' he said. 'Come with me. We're leaving.'

He dragged Icarus back to their room, and began tearing the shirt off his back and daubing him with a warm, white, thick, glutinous mess. All the while, the boy protested, 'I don't want to go anywhere. I like it here. What is this? Get it off me. It stinks!'

'It's candle wax. I've been collecting up the candle stubs after supper for six months,' said his father. Throwing open a chest in the corner of the room, he brought out, with reverent care, what looked like two dead eagles. 'I hoped it would never come to this,' said Daedalus.

Icarus was so startled by the beauty of the feathers when the wings were spread that he did not speak as his father plastered his own naked back with molten wax and struggled to mount a pair of wings. 'Well, don't just stand gaping, boy. Help me. It's difficult, behind my back.'

'You look like a duck,' said Icarus, chiefly out of fright.

'If I fly like one, I shan't mind,' said Daedalus, attaching a great drooping span of wings, each threaded out of thousands of feathers, to his son's shoulders. 'Now. These thongs on the leading edge are for your hands. Don't flap. Birds don't flap. Just leap, and let the hot air thermals carry you up high before you cross the coastline and move out to sea.'

Icarus took in none of this. He had just caught sight of his reflection in a bronze ewer on the table and was turning this way and that, with his wings spread, to appreciate the rainbow of oily colours in them. 'Above all, Icarus, above all, you must not fly too close to the sun. If we go now, in the cool of the morning, we shall be over the mainland by the time the sun's at its hottest.

If the gods had meant us to fly, they would have allowed the birds to share the secret of flight with us. But I've studied the birds. I've copied their wings. I've made what, till now, only the gods could have made. So keep low—out of reach of the sun's heat, or the wax will melt on your shoulders, and no god will reach out a hand to catch you as you fall.'

Icarus was at the window, gazing out in the direction of the distant sea. The new palace was tall and built on the edge of an escarpment, so that the drop below the window-sill made him dizzy with fear. A handful of busy sparrows hopped on and off the ledge, fluttering out over the drop; their tittering twittering was like an insult.

'I don't want to go. I like it here,' said Icarus, whiningly.

'Even though the king has said he'll feed you to the Minotaur? Now, jump, boy! Don't you want to be the first person in the history of the world to fly?'

Whether Daedalus unbalanced his son as he leapt past him, or whether Icarus jumped to stop his father going first, neither was sure. But after a moment's tumbling and an explosion of loose, ungluing feathers, the wind jammed under their wings with a bone-jarring shock, and they ceased to fall.

Air coming in off the sea and meeting the warm land, swept up the escarpment in columns, and on this hot air Daedalus and Icarus stalled and hovered. Their fists were white and their muscles knotted at first with unnecessary effort, but gradually they relaxed, and the island beneath them became like a carpet, a beautifully intricate carpet hung against a blue-painted wall of sea. They dipped a wing and turned away from Crete, out over the ocean, towards Sicily.

Daedalus was thinking, The seagull feathers are good. I shouldn't have bothered with the finches. Eagle

46

feathers would be best, of course—but so hard to come by . . .

Icarus was thinking, The first person to fly! That's what I am! What would the Princess Ariadne say if she could see me now. Look, a ship! I've a mind to sweep by their mast! They'll mistake me for the god Hermes himself. What? My wings are ten times the size of his! Ten times greater than a god! I don't need to squat on Olympus and bow down to Zeus every morning. I could fly straight over the peak of Olympus and pull Zeus's beard! I could cut the reins of the sun-god's chariot and send it careering all over the sky. What's to stop me? I could race the sun from horizon to horizon! I'll challenge him!

Down on the ship which Icarus had sighted, the Prince Theseus looked up and glimpsed the distant shapes of two birds against the bright sky. Too bright to discern what breed of bird, but one was much higher than the other, and spiralling higher still, towards the unwatchable sun. But Theseus's mind was on his destination and the thirteen companions who, with him, were being shipped as tributes to the king of Crete—as sacrifices to the hideous Minotaur.

'Not so high! Not so high!' cried Daedalus, though his son was already out of hailing distance. 'Remember what I told you! The heat of the sun, boy! *The heat of the sun!*'

Shreds of sound did reach Icarus, but ambition and pride had so swelled inside him—like dry bread inside a little bird—that he hardly felt the need of wings on his back. He felt he could have flown without them. The air was thin, too; it set his head spinning and stifled any common sense. It made him dizzy and hysterical.

Way, way above Icarus, the sun looked over the side of his blazing chariot and saw the tiny speck of a figure ascending. Not a bird—for the birds had long since learned that there was nothing to be gained from climbing so high—not another god, for none of the Immortals would have made himself look so ridiculous, daubed with wax and stuck with motley feathers. The sun reined in his chariot in a moment's astonishment, and sparks flew from around the incandescent wheel-rims. Heat pulsed and radiated from its blazing gold, like the ripples from a splash; the air throbbed with an unbreathable, searing heat. 'Little upstart!' snorted the sun-god, leaning out over the side of his chariot to keep Icarus in sight. The celestial horses paced and tugged in the traces, impatient to reach their stables below the western horizon. The chariot moved on, but still its waves of heat washed over Icarus's head.

There was no room in his lungs for boasting, now— only the thin, singeing air. There was no room in his heart for pride—only the pumping of terror. There were no wings on his back, either—only the larding trickle of wax as it melted and dripped and dropped.

Theseus shielded his eyes with one hand, against the brightness of the noonday sun, and saw a shape fall out of the sky and splash into the sea. A sea eagle diving for fish, perhaps. Another such shape was descending, in slower, sweeping turns, towards the settling spray. But the scar in the water had been already rubbed out by the incessant rolling of the sea. Theseus shrugged. His mind was on his mother who had died of plague because of him. 'Time to get into your costumes,' he said to his fellow sacrifices. 'Crete must be just over the horizon.'

* * *

Daedalus flew to and fro, to and fro until, at last, the body of his only son rose from the depths to which it had plunged. He scooped it from the water as a fish-eagle clasps a fish, and flew on to Sicily. A scorched and waxy pair of wings fluttered down a great while later, and washed about on the waves like a huge, dead bird.

7

Admiring Women

'I feel a fool,' said one of the young men. He was wearing a long, blonde wig and a gown stuffed out with sponge and cork.

'Better to look a fool and be a gentleman than to look a gentleman and be a fool,' said Theseus. Instead of seven men and seven maids, he had brought with him from Athens thirteen young men. He refused, Oracle or no Oracle, to allow young women to be fed to the Minotaur. 'Think of your sister and the fate you've saved her from,' he told the young man in the wig.

Theseus, in his pride, was not surprised to find King Minos himself awaiting the boat's arrival in the harbour at Heraklion. But Minos had actually come there in pursuit of his inventor, thinking that he must have fled the island by boat. Having found no trace of Daedalus or Icarus, the king was in a furious temper. He decided to comfort himself by gloating over the tribute from Athens. He would feed the first sacrifices to the Minotaur that night: the entertainment would take his mind off Daedalus. So there he was, on the dockside, when

Theseus's ship berthed. Standing at the prow were seven sturdy and buxom women. One had a particularly fine figure.

Daedalus and Icarus were suddenly forgotten as Minos tugged smugly at his beard and leered. 'You! Young woman! What would you say to a better fate than the horns of the Minotaur? Give me your hand and step ashore, won't you?' The young woman looked in panic towards Theseus, and stood rooted to the deck. 'Come on! Come on!' coaxed King Minos. 'Don't be frightened. I like to have big women around me. It's a stupid woman who turns down the chance to live.'

'Then Athens is full of stupid women, Minos!' cried Theseus. 'Our young women would rather die than lose their honour to a Cretan dog!'

King Minos's mouth fell open into a kind of fascinated grin. 'So! You must be Theseus. I heard that you volunteered to be one of the sacrifices. Such an honourable act deserves a just reward. What shall it be? I know! *You* shall be first into the Labyrinth!'

A young woman had been moving slowly along the waterfront, towards the king. She limped slightly, and carried her shoulders high in awkward nervousness. But she was dressed with the elegant simplicity of a rich woman and, as she walked, she nervously fingered a golden bracelet that snaked round her arm. Her eyes took in the Athenian boat and its cargo.

She reached the king's side at the moment he was taunting Theseus with the prospect of death in the Labyrinth; she fumbled at the bracelet and it fell to the ground and rolled into the deep harbour. King Minos turned furiously and slapped the girl. 'How careless, Ariadne. Clumsy and careless as usual. What are you doing here? Why aren't you at the palace?'

The girl blushed and her lip trembled as she stared

into the water. 'I saw the black sail . . . the Athenian ship . . . and I just . . . thought I'd just . . . '

'You wanted to see the famous Theseus, I suppose,' sneered the king. 'Well, take a good look. Famous broad shoulders; famous yellow hair; famous blue eyes. They say those eyes prove that he's the son of Poseidon himself! Tomorrow he'll be wandering through the Labyrinth, and the smell of him will be in the Minotaur's nose.'

'I am not the son of Poseidon, madam,' said Theseus loudly, 'but I'll fetch back your bracelet from the realm of Poseidon!' And in a gesture of great chivalry, he leapt over the side of the boat and disappeared from view.

It was a grand gesture, but once in the water, Theseus had not the smallest idea how to find the princess's bracelet. Instead of a firm, sandy bottom lit by filtered beams of sunlight, the harbour had a muddy bottom scattered with refuse and cloudy with fish offal. As he poked about with outstretched fingers, his feet flailing above his head, more and more silt swirled off the seabed, and the water grew more and more turbid. He swam straight into the loop of a ship's cable, and thought how ignominious it would be to hang himself accidentally, underwater, in some foreign port. He had a particular dislike of eels and crabs and starfish and all the other things that crawl in the sea's mud.

So when, in the murk, something soft pressed against his face, he loosed a cry of bubbles that almost emptied him of air. Then he saw that the softness was the flank of a grey-blue dolphin, and in its beak was the bracelet. But when Theseus took hold of its splayed tail, it dragged him not to the surface, but between a maze of boat-keels and out of the harbour mouth.

Just once it surfaced—long enough for him to gulp in air—and then it plunged down and down and down into a sea trench, to where the water was not warmed or much lit by the sun, and the only colour was the turquoise roof of the sea's surface far above. Under a canopy of barnacle-covered rock, tasselled with scarlet seaweed and hung with the sail of a sunken ship, sat the queen of the mermaids. She held a conversation, in clicks and squeaks, with the dolphin, during which the princess's golden bracelet dropped to the sand. But Theseus, whose eyes were bulging and whose lungs were collapsing for want of air, could only point to it and throw up his hands in a slow-motion helplessness.

After the mermaid kissed him on the mouth, it was as if he had taken three deep breaths in the dry sunlight.

She said very little that he could understand and her voice was dolphin-like, peppered with sharp clickings of her tongue. But Theseus quickly realized that she *approved* of him: 'Beautiful! Enchanting! Almost godlike!' Her tail encircled his legs like a tongue, licking. Languorously she wound herself around him, tail first and her long arms trailing. Her hair coiled about his head and neck. The dolphin thrust the bracelet back into his protesting hands and the queen of the mermaids thrust her crown on to Theseus's head. 'Delicious! Incomparable!' And with a clicking in her throat like the teeth of a comb, she went spiralling out of sight through a fountain of bubbles threshed from the water by her massive fins.

The dolphin stood on its tail, backing away from Theseus in a series of bows, like an obsequious courtier. It was beckoning him to follow and, catching hold of its tail again, he was swept back through the harbour mouth, back through the maze of boat-keels, to the weed-slimy wall of the waterfront.

When his head burst into the open air, Theseus could hear the sound of oars splashing, swords rattling and the double-quick march of soldiers running. His dive had been mistaken for an attempt to escape, and Minos was shamed by the prince's gallant return and the presents of crown and bracelet that he laid at Princess Ariadne's feet. The look on the girl's face was charming to see; her lips were pursed as if to open them would have spilled all the admiration inside. Her eyes shone.

But all the other Athenians had been bound with rope and loaded into an open cart, like provender on its way to market. Theseus was forced to join them.

The size of Crete astonished Theseus. As he had sailed into harbour, the island had reached out on either side as far as the eye could see. What people called an island seemed to Theseus like a continent, and more buildings perched on it than seagulls on a rock.

On the journey inland, it began to rain—a cold, persistent drizzle that soaked the prisoners through and through and saturated their disguises. They plucked at their plaits, nervous of being found out. But their guards rode heads-down in the rain.

At first, Theseus memorized each crossroad, each notable tree, each farm building they passed. But the journey to Knossos palace was so long that he soon lost his sense of direction. If he escaped now, he would not know which way to run for the sea. 'Still, it's an island,' he told himself. 'Whichever way I go, I shall find the sea.'

The landscape was strangely green compared with dry Troezen or sunbaked Athens. He resolved one day that Athens must conquer Crete and seize its fertile farms and fat cattle. But it was an arrogant hope. Everything on Crete was so new, so remarkable, that it was like stepping forward into a future time.

And when he saw Knossos palace, his confidence for the first time failed him. Here was a building the like of which he had never seen—so beautiful that even the young men doomed to die in its cellars were glad to have seen it. Its pillars were spirals of marble, and its walls shone with blue waves, like the sea itself, with playing dolphins and leaping acrobats, charging bulls and scroll patterns high and low. Most remarkable of all was the sheer size of the palace which was not (like the buildings of Athens) made up of four walls and a roof, but was three- and four-storeys high. Stairs—not ladders but stairs cut like terraces in a mountainside—climbed up to rooms balanced *on top* of the ones below! And stairs went *down*, too, into chambers and cells cut like caves out of the ground itself! There were not two corridors but a dozen, not four windows but forty. This fantastical palace, built with skills that were nowhere to be found in Athens, towered over Theseus and made envy stir in the pit of his stomach. To see all this and then to die without a chance to copy it? That would be too galling to bear.

'What made me think of that?' Theseus demanded of himself. 'What made me think of dying? I killed Poseidon's bull, didn't I? So I can cut its monstrous son into joints of beef, can't I?'

The high gutters of the palace spilled rainwater on his head, and he shivered convulsively. 'It's a wet day I'm having!' he called out loudly to his companions. 'A man could catch his death of cold!' The prisoners smiled wanly at him as they were jabbed and prodded with spears, and hurried through the huge doors, down stone steps and into the palace jail.

It grew dark outside without Minos sending for a sacrifice. A Cretan sailor had arrived at Knossos with news of Daedalus and Icarus. He had seen them, he said, *flying* towards the mainland, and had followed their flight for as long as he was able, in his caique. A short while after losing sight of them, he had found a huge pair of wings washing about in the ocean. One at least had drowned. From their cell in the cellars, the Athenian prisoners could hear the king laughing out loud—a hollow, sinister, echoing laugh that set the beast in the Labyrinth bellowing. And the bellowing went on all night. The Minotaur had not been fed, and it was hungry for meat and marrowjuice.

8

The Beast in the Labyrinth

Minos did not send for Theseus first, after all. In the morning, one of the young men was dragged to the door by the guards, kicking and screaming. He clutched at Theseus, who stood beside the door. 'You said *you'd* go first. You didn't say it would be like this. You said we wouldn't have to die!' Theseus shrugged and turned his face to the wall, and they heard the struggle continue in the corridor overhead—further on, the scraping of a grid, the thump as the boy was dropped through, the rattle of the grid sliding back into place. There was a sobbing and scuffle of feet as the boy ran, through the pitch black corridors, away—or so he hoped—from the Minotaur.

When Theseus turned back to face his companions, they were staring at him with pale, shocked faces. 'He was right. You did say you'd go first,' said the boldest of them.

'I wasn't sent for.'

'You could have offered.'

'Well, of course I could! But think! You're quick enough with your reproaches, but you're so slow to *think*! It's *morning*. If we're to escape, we need cover of

57

darkness. It's no good my fighting the Minotaur until this evening.'

The boys nodded sheepishly; all except one who muttered, 'He could have killed the Minotaur and stayed hidden till evening.' They all put their hands over their ears as they heard the first sacrifice turn a corner and meet, in the blackness, the Minotaur.

At noon, the Princess Ariadne brought the prison guards their lunches. They were startled to see the royal princess in such a low part of the palace, but she explained that she wanted to make the prisoners beg for their lives: it would be fun, she said, to refuse them. Once outside the cell gate, she signalled urgently to Theseus and he went closer to the door. Ariadne said, 'Theseus, if I help you to escape, will you take me with you?—As your wife?' Theseus looked round sharply, but none of his companions had heard.

Escape. What a sweet sound the word had to it, all of a sudden! Escape! Then Theseus remembered the boy in the Labyrinth. 'I came here to kill the Minotaur. I won't go back until it's dead.'

She was taken aback, but after running her eyes up and down his body she said, 'You might. You just might. But what then? How will you find your way out of the Labyrinth without my help? Nobody does, you know. Nobody ever has. It's a maze, you see. Daedalus built it so that a man could wander up and down its passageways for forty years and never find his way back to the grid.'

'But you know the secret?' Now it was Theseus's turn to run his eyes up and down Ariadne.

He did not much like what he saw. She strongly resembled her father and she stood awkwardly, with one hip stuck out, so that both feet could rest flat on the floor. They were large feet. Her hair had neither the ambition to curl nor the weight to hang straight. Her eyes, which doted on Theseus, were pleasant, however. So was her mouth which, as his eyes lighted on it, opened and said, 'I love you, Theseus. I loved you the first moment I saw you. I loved you before, when I heard the stories they told about you. And I love you now.'

'And I love you, too, Ariana.'

'Ariadne.'

'Ariadne. Why else did I leap into the sea to get back your bracelet? Why else did I beg the queen of mermaids to give me her crown as a present for you? Why wouldn't I count myself honoured above all men if I could take you with me when I leave here. Now . . . what's the secret of the Labyrinth?'

'Open your hand.'

He opened his hand and, furtively, she thrust something into it—something harsh and small and round.

'A ball of string?' he said, with a look on his face that was something between disbelief and disgust. And what was more, she took it back!

The guards came, then, and warned the princess not to stand so near the grille, in case the prisoners took it into their heads to grab at her. She hurried away, bobbing as she limped, and lifting her dress on the stairs, so that her big feet showed. As she went, she glanced over her shoulder at Theseus. Crying made her mouth less pretty than before.

Theseus was sent for at suppertime—escorted to the king's chamber and searched thoroughly for any kind of weapon. The chamber was full of evening sunlight and beautiful women whose dresses plunged to their waists and were caught up between their legs. These were the bull-maidens of Crete, the acrobats who leapt the horns of charging bulls and rode standing upright on their withers. At the sight of them, Theseus was filled with a longing to live. If he, the prince of Athens, was to marry such a brave Cretan beauty, what children might come of it! The thought kept his mind off the bellowing in the cellar.

'I have seen him,' declared King Minos. 'I have looked my last on the mighty Prince Theseus and so has the world! Take him away and feed him to my beast!'

Theseus shook off the guards' hands and walked, of his own free will, back down the corridors to the open grid of the Labyrinth. He would not let them lay hands on him or throw him into the darkness, but hopped lightly down and landed on his feet.

'Don't worry!' he shouted out, knowing his companions would be able to hear him from their prison cell. 'I'll be back!' Then the grid rattled back into place over his head and he was alone in the Labyrinth with the darkness and the Minotaur.

But there was Ariadne's ball of string, one end tied to the grid, and the ball lying by his feet. All he had to do was hold it in one hand as he went, and let it unwind and ravel out behind him. Whenever he chose, he could follow it back the way he had come. 'Of course! Why didn't I think of that? So simple. A clever lady, that princess,' mused Theseus.

At every bend in the Labyrinth, there were two choices of passage. For every choice there were four more choices beyond. At first, Theseus knew when the prison cells were behind him, when the king's chamber was overhead. But after a time, he felt like a child that has been blindfolded and whirled round and round and round and left to blunder, hands outstretched, in search of someone to touch. Sometimes the ceiling was so low he felt he was suffocating. Sometimes passageways led off

round him in eight different directions, and he felt he
was lashed to the hub of a giant wheel that was spinning,
spinning, spinning. When he fell over something in the
dark, he scarcely knew which was the floor, which was
the wall, which was the ceiling. His reaching hands
discovered what he had fallen over. Yesterday it had been
a young Athenian. Today it was no longer.

'I am Theseus. Prince of Athens!' He heard his voice, thin
and high-pitched, dribbling away down the passages like
water down a sewer. It came trickling back, distorted and
redoubled, from the passageway behind him. The hair
stood up on the nape of his neck. His scalp crawled. And
he set off to run, colliding with brick walls, falling over
mounds of bones, flaying the skin off his hands as he
turned invisible corners.

One more corner, and he found himself dazzled by
the meagre light of one torch jammed into a bracket on
the wall. A figure—it seemed to be a man in hide
trousers and no shirt—was bending over a manger of
straw, his back to the doorway. As Theseus blundered
into the core of the Labyrinth, the figure straightened up
and turned to face him.

'So you have come at last. I have been waiting for
you, Theseus of Athens,' said the Minotaur.

It was a soft, lowing voice, and the eyes which
fastened on Theseus's sweating face were liquid brown
and full of reflections of the burning torch. Huge, velvety
nostrils rankled at the smell of him. The hinder hooves
clattered on the paved floor. The string fell from Theseus's
hand and rolled away, back into the darkness. 'You killed
my father, and now you have come here to destroy me.
Well. We shall see. We shall see.'

Theseus heard himself saying, 'Yes, beast—monster—
murderer. Yes, we shall see.'

The beast spread his hands to either side of his darkly

61

haired body and shrugged. 'I am a man encased in the nature of a bull; I am an animal cursed with the vices of a man. I am a beast imprisoned for ever in the dark horrors of the Labyrinth. What is your excuse, young man?'

But Theseus, seeking the element of surprise, snatched the torch out of its bracket, and flung it at the Minotaur. It ducked aside, and the torch fell into the manger, where flames flared up with a deafening roar and threw fifty gigantic shadows of the Minotaur across the tiny cell. The beast reached out a calm, unpanicked hand and took Theseus by the throat, lowering its head to gore with one horn.

By the light of the blazing straw, they struggled on the floor of the cell, grappling for holds, biting and wrenching and kicking. They drove the breath out of one another in great sobs and groans. There was none of the skill or finesse of wrestling. There was none of the flourish of a bullfight—just a desperate, grappling mêlée of fists and hooves and horns and feet. Theseus could not get a grip on the shining hide. The Minotaur could not keep hold of Theseus for the quantity of sweat that ran down him. The beast had hold of his wrist, and pinned him to the floor; a horn tore open his shoulder. Theseus broke free and threw hot ash into the beast's moist eyes. He wrenched the red hot manger off the wall, and branded the Minotaur's hide so that the creature bellowed in torment and fell to its knees.

Then Theseus had hold of the horns—just as he had taken hold of the blue bull's horns—and wrenched them round and down. The bull-man was reaching over its shoulders, clawing for some counter-hold on Theseus's body. Suddenly it let its arms drop and said, 'You were always my fate. Oh! to be gone from here!'

Theseus threw his whole weight on the horns, and

the Minotaur fell dead beneath him, its neck broken and its eyes closed, as if in sleep. Large drops of moisture sparkled on the muzzle: the ashes had enflamed its eyes, Theseus supposed.

Presently, the last straw burned itself out, and utter blackness closed in. Theseus crawled about the floor of the cell, the breath sobbing in his throat, groping, groping for the ball of twine. What was that noise? Did the beast stir? Was it not entirely dead? Theseus swept his hands frantically over the paving slabs and, at last, brushed against the string Ariadne had given him. It rolled away from him, and it seemed hours more before he found it again. Clutching it to him, he began, on hands and knees, to wind up the ravelled string. It led him—along a route that defied all logic—left and right and round and round the maze of Daedalus's Labyrinth. It was more intricate than a spider's web, more complex than the blood vessels in a man's hand. It had as many tricks and turns to it as the cunning brain of its architect.

Then Theseus looked up and saw Ariadne's face above him, beyond the bars of the grid, holding the end of the string, and he burst out with joyful gratitude: 'I love you, Ariadne of Knossos! I love you!'

She was muffled up in her cloak, ready for the journey. 'Quickly! Quickly!' she kept saying. 'We must get away from here. If my father finds out that I'm gone, we'll never get off the island.'

But Theseus would not go without his twelve companions. He killed the sleeping guards and opened the prison gate. Together, all fourteen of them—as many leaving as had come—crept out of Knossos Palace to the horses Ariadne had stationed in readiness. 'I have a boat in the river estuary below Margarites,' she said.

'What colour is the sail?' said Theseus.

'What colour is the sail? What kind of a question is that? I don't know . . . brown, I think.'

'Then it won't do. We'll go back to Heraklion and leave aboard the boat we came in. There's a white sail rolled up under the decks. I promised my father the king that I'd send the ship home under its black sail if I failed, and sail it home under a white one if I succeeded. He'll be watching for a white sail, you see.'

So, despite the extra risk, despite the lights that burned in braziers along the waterfront and the coming and going of little fishing boats in the harbour, Theseus and his crew and the Princess Ariadne crept to the prow of their Athenian ship, and slipped the cables which moored it.

Then Theseus sent one youth to each of the Cretan fighting ships moored to the marble waterfront. On board each ship they left fuses burning—little orange glows in the darkness. As the Athenian ship under its black sail slipped out of Heraklion harbour, the glow of dawn increased and the orange glow of fuses in the fighting ships grew to a great inferno of burning timber and canvas and rope. Lights came up in the houses, too—the hundreds of houses perched like seagulls on a rock— and all the town came running to see the king's fleet sink in flames to the bottom of the harbour.

9

Ariadne

There were no bounds to Ariadne's joy. Although she had left behind her mother, her father, and the island where she had been born, nothing could dim her delight. She wore it like the shining cloak that hid her twisted leg, her clumsy body, and her large feet. Tending to Theseus's wounds at the hands of the Minotaur, she felt she could just as easily have mended the rift in the clouds where the sun shone through. Preparing him a meal on board, she felt she could have made wine out of water and bread out of sand. Standing at the prow of his ship and looking out for a first glimpse of mainland Hellas, she felt she could have streaked there through the waves like a blue dolphin, guided by the stars. If Poseidon's great blue bull had come now, hurtling over the waves to smash the little ship to fragments, she could have cartwheeled over its back and ridden on its shoulders all the way to Athens—and better than any bull-maiden of Crete! She was loved, and she was overflowing with love herself.

It amused Theseus to see her standing there at the prow of the ship, leaning forward over the water while, below her, the ship shouldered aside the sea. But the crew sniggered and said, 'Seen prettier figureheads, eh, Lord Theseus?'

Into her cloak, Ariadne had stitched so many valuables—jewellery and money—that every hour she could produce some new and precious present for Theseus, like a conjuror producing birds. But the young men giggled as they whispered together. 'It's just as well she has got treasure inside that cloak of hers, because she hasn't much else to interest Theseus.'

Ariadne was an educated and sensible woman—she knew more than Theseus did about the lands beyond Crete. She amazed them all with stories of a nation to the East peopled by tall, swarthy women who waged war as warriors while their menfolk stayed at home to cook and tend the animals. But it only made the young men rub their hands eagerly and say, 'That's the kind of wife for me! I'll stay home and she can go out and do the work!'

Theseus, too, thought, That's the kind of wife I need—some handsome warrior-woman who would give me sons like Hercules and fight back-to-back with me against the enemies of Athens. Yes, I could be happy with a woman like that.

That was when he began to look at Ariadne out of the corner of his eye, to watch her as she moved about the boat, but without letting her see that he was watching. When she turned to look at him, he made a point of looking another way. He did not choose to meet her eye: something about the shortness of her lashes depressed him.

They put in at the island of Naxos for fresh water. Ariadne went and picked fresh limes to make a cordial for Theseus. She milked a goat and brought him the cream. She offered to scrub down his white sail which had got stained in the bilges to a dirty brown.

'These are not the pastimes of a princess,' said Theseus.

'No, but they are things I can do to please you, and that is why it pleases me to do them,' she said, and struggled down the gangplank, dragging the white sail after her.

But Ariadne did *not* please Theseus by fetching and carrying, by working and thinking of work to do. All his life he had imagined himself marrying a woman with all the regal dignity of the rising sun, with all the stately splendour of noonday, with all the beauty of sunset. He looked for pride in her, equal to his own pride. Hour by hour, since leaving the Labyrinth, he found that he loved Ariadne less and less. By the time they reached Naxos, he loved her not at all.

Their marriage bargain was still a secret. None of the young men knew what he had promised. Ariadne had picked up the ball of string at the mouth of the Labyrinth and said that he must carry it with him always, as a token of her love. 'You have entangled my heart in a maze,' she said, 'and in an endless cord of love.'

The young men were adamant: they would not sail back into the king's presence in the dresses and wigs of their disguises. So they ripped them into long shreds and ran howling and whooping into the nearest village to steal clothes from the local men. Ariadne, quiet and industrious, was down by the water's edge in a little bay near the harbour, but out of sight of the ship. Theseus leaned back from the waist and threw the ball of twine as far out to sea as his strength would let him. It hit the seam of the horizon that joins the sky to the sea.

When Theseus's men came running back from the village, they were anxious to get under way. Theseus had only to cut the cable and let the boat blow out to sea on a stiffening off-shore breeze . . .

When Ariadne saw it sail round the head of the bay, her hands hovered over the sailcloth she had been scrubbing. She could see Theseus standing at the prow, his face towards the horizon. She raised one arm to signal, and shouted his name.

But he neither turned his head nor looked for who had called. His name broke off in Ariadne's throat, like a fishbone that choked her, and she let her hand fall. The surf rolled over the white sail and washed it away from her, into deeper water. But Ariadne stood watching the ship move away. The further it sailed, the smaller it seemed to grow, and inside Ariadne's narrow chest, her heart shrank too, until it was only a small, black speck.

When Theseus saw what he had done and how easily he had done it, he dusted his hands together and grinned at his good fortune.

Then the thunder rolled among the mountains of the gods, and a soughing roar came from the sea. The smile froze on Theseus's face, and he looked over his shoulder, suddenly convinced that he was being watched.

The great black square of the sail flapped at him . . . like a fragment of night that had snagged on the mast as they sailed out of Heraklion harbour . . . like a fragment of nightmare.

'Where's the white sail?' he said, as the mainland came into view.

King Aegeus's advisers and courtiers tried to tell him that Theseus might be gone for weeks—months—that King Minos might keep him in chains for a long, long while before sending him into the Labyrinth. But Aegeus knew Minos's lust for blood, and the Minotaur's ravenous appetite. 'By the third day Theseus will either be dead or he will be sailing home from Crete,' he told them. Then he went and stood on the clifftops to watch for the returning ship.

Up there on the cliffs, with the sea below him and the sounds of the city drowned by the gulls, Aegeus realized how little he cared about being a king. His wife had died of the plague, and now his only son, his Theseus, was pitting his life against the terror of the world. Aegeus wished he could have been a farmer, with one or two sheep and a little son with thin arms and legs and not many brains, who stayed home from morning till night.

He prayed, 'O you gods, look down on Theseus wherever he is. Judge what a fine boy he is, and reward me with his safe return! It's not true what the Oracle said! He didn't bring me grief—not really—he never made me sorry to have a son. If he returns home to me, I'll give up my crown and trust Athens to his safe-keeping. O grant it, you immortal gods, and I shall be at peace for ever. *Send a white sail! Oh, please!*'

Over the horizon it came, like a small black tear in the seascape. Aegeus tried to tell himself that it was another ship, a different ship, not an Athenian ship at all. But the closer it came, the more certain it was: Theseus's ship was sailing home beneath a black sail. He had failed.

Aegeus sank to his knees and rocked slowly to and fro. His face was quite empty of expression. He said, 'Now it's true. Now. The Oracle did speak the truth. ''If you have a son,'' she said, ''he'll bring you sorrow.'' And here it comes—a ship laden with a cargo of sorrow enough to fill all the storehouses of Athens. You were right, Xenoclea. Rather than live through this moment, I would sooner have had no son. Well. Well, I'll not go down to the harbour and off-load that cargo of sorrow. No. Let Athens find a new king. There will always be

69

kings enough to fill the world's crowns. There will never be another Theseus . . . And there will be no more King Aegeus.'

And raising his arms over his head, he let himself fall forward over the edge of the cliff, into the roaring protests of the sea's open mouth.

10

Hippolyta, Queen of the Amazons

E very officer of state, every general of the army, every lady-in-waiting and all the children of the palace were aboard the black galley which put out from Pyrrheus that day. King Theseus was at the prow, raised up on a gilded platform and standing knee-deep in flowers. They sailed along the sword-bright channel of reflected light that stretched across the sea from the rising sun, and when they had rowed ten leagues, the oarsmen drew in their oars.

'Because this sea holds my father's body, let it be called for evermore the Aegean Sea, in memory of him.' Theseus lifted a wreath of flowers off the platform and pitched it into the sea. Flower petals drifted away like the feathers of a drowned bird.

An approving murmur ran round the ship; statesmen nodded and said that it had been well done, very well done, and their ladies agreed with them. Then a child, who had climbed up the empty rigging for a better view, called out that there were sails to the north.

'And to the south, too.'

'And some behind us!'

71

'And more sailing out of the sun!'

They were beautiful, junk-rigged sails, woven in orange and flame-red, and worked with strange symbols. Each ship had eyes painted to either side of the prow which swept up like an arm raised in salute.

In his pride, Theseus thought that the news of his conquest of the Minotaur and his sinking of the Cretan fleet had brought this convoy from the far side of the ocean to pay tribute to his bravery. Only when the flotilla of gleaming ships had circled the black galley and they were turning in to ram her did he realize, too late.

'They're Amazonian ships!'

Beyond the shields that decorated the sails of the bright hulls, beyond the flash of spearheads, the hair of the crew was curled as tightly as the fleece of a black lamb and their bodies gleamed with oil. Tall they were— taller than all but Theseus, and their teeth flashed white in their black faces, and their armour flashed, here and there, where it was fastened with silver clasps.

Two or three aboard Theseus's galley were armed with bow and arrows. But they hesitated as they drew back their bowstrings, and the arrowheads wavered on their fists. 'They're *women*, my lord Theseus!'

'Yes—women in body, but lions inwardly! These are the Amazons! You gods on Olympus, were you *sleeping* to let heathens get the better of Athens like this? And *women*, too!'

'Have a care,' whispered his chief-lieutenant. 'The goddess Athene, guardian of Athens, is a woman in armour.'

Theseus opened his mouth in retort, but only snarled in exasperation as he looked around him. The ladies-in-waiting were shrieking up and down the galley. The children were crying. Officials of state were fighting each other over who should hide in the sail locker. The army generals had not loosed a single arrow.

On came the eyed ships, the high-prowed, high, proud, Amazonian ships, and the black galley lay helpless. Theseus drew his sword and waited for the splintering of wood that would come when they rammed him.

But the Amazonian ships carried brake-oarsmen— women of gigantic size who could stop the progress of their craft within three strokes of an oar. The warlike bows halted, with their painted eyes gazing over the rails of the funeral galley, and a woman's voice put a sudden end to the Athenian panic:

'Theseus! Prince of Athens! Surrender to an enemy who has you by the throat!'

Having no plan, and no hope of winning a fight, Theseus sought to delay his surrender. 'Prince? Your spies are slow to inform you, Amazon! I am King Theseus now! May a king not ask to speak with the leader of those who would rob him of his crown?'

There was a pause and then a woman as tall as Theseus himself and dressed in armour just as fine as his own, leapt the tall bow of her ship and landed on the stern deck, scattering a huddle of maidens. 'I am Hippolyta, Queen of the Amazons. Which is Theseus?'

The blood stirred in Theseus's veins when he saw Queen Hippolyta striding towards him down the length of the boat. She moved like the oily black water of an African river. Her arms were like the massively entwined creepers of the jungle, and her hips were as wide as the bole of a baobab tree. Her throat was as dark and inviting as the wine flowing from a wineskin, and her lips seemed swollen from eating succulent and exotic fruits. He drew in a sharp breath of admiration, and reached down a hand to help her on to the flower-strewn platform.

Looking up into his face, she missed her footing and fell against him as she landed, and he wrapped steadying arms around her. 'Queen Hippolyta, my shame is

73

deserved, since before now I neglected to invite the world's most beautiful woman to be a guest in the city-state of Athens.'

She leaned back from him, like a rearing cobra. 'So, you are Theseus, who slew the Minotaur and scuttled the Minoan fleet. Is it true, then, that your father was your so-called sea god, Poseidon?'

'Not a word. I am as mortal as you are!' and Theseus laughed.

'Can mortal eyes be so blue?' she said.

'Yours eclipse them with their darkness.'

'Or mortal hair so bright?'

'In the eyes of our gods, black lambs are a more perfect sacrifice than white ones.'

'Would you have put me to the sword, then, like a lamb, if you had conquered me in battle?'

'Lady! I slew the Minotaur and Sciron and the Crommyonian Boar. But what kind of a fool would I be to cut the brightest star out of the sky? My sword would sooner have melted.'

'Oh, Theseus!'

There was a long silence full of glances and sighs, before Theseus took the queen's fleecy head between his hands and kissed her on the mouth.

'Empty the boat,' she murmured, and when Theseus was slow to respond, she pulled out of his arms and shouted to her women, 'I want this boat empty! Ferry the Athenians home safely and allow them to give you food and drink and entertainment.'

Her warrior maidens were astounded. 'But Queen Hippolyta! We have them at our mercy. Shan't we stick them with our spears?'

'No! I have surrendered to King Theseus. He is the victor, I tell you. Deliver yourselves into the hands of his generals. I command it. And empty this boat.'

So all the officers of state, the generals in the army, ladies-in-waiting, and children of the palace were lifted over the gunwales into the Amazonian ships and ferried ashore. Amazonian and Athenian were each as astonished as the other, exchanging suspicious glances. Theseus and Hippolyta were left drifting in the black galley, in the heart of the Aegean Sea, amid flowers, and under a blazing sun. It was three days before they re-entered Pyrrheus harbour below Athens.

Hippolyta sent her women home. She gave away her crown to her sister, saying that she had no more heart to live by fighting, and that the Amazons had a new queen now.

'But what will become of you?' asked her sister.

'I shall stay here with my Theseus.'

'But are you to be married? We'll stay for the wedding! Shall you be queen of Athens? We'll ally ourselves to these Athenians and fight by their sides in war!'

'In time. All in good time,' said Hippolyta smiling the distant, thoughtful smile that was new to her. 'What marriage can there be? In front of which altar would we take vows—he in front of the altar of Pallas Athene and I in the sight of my ancestors? I consider that we are married already—since I am going to have his child.'

So soon there were only two black lambs left among the white flocks of Athens: Hippolyta and her baby son, Hippolyte. They brought as much beauty to the city as a verse of poetry written in black ink on a scroll of white paper. When she shed her armour and wore Athenian robes, the people stopped trembling at the sight of her and began to admire her graceful movements, her graceful dealings, her graceful words and laughter. And as Hippolyte grew up, there were those who greeted him in the streets with the words, 'Hail to the prince of Athens.'

Hippolyta was like Theseus's shadow, always at his heel in the morning, and dancing when the lamplight flickered in the evening. Her love was as edgeless as the night. And just as a man ceases to notice his own shadow, Theseus hardly gave her a thought.

Oh, she was a pretty enough ornament in his palace. And Hippolyte, at two years old, was life itself to Theseus. His skin was the colour of acacia honey, and his hair was like the Golden Fleece. But his mother was nothing to Theseus, who thought of her as a prize he had won in battle—a trophy awarded him by the gods, out of admiration.

In his pride, Theseus did not notice that his own bright hair was greying, that his own tanned skin was lined with age and that heroes, when there are no monsters left to fight, grow old like ordinary men.

And ordinary men fall in love.

Love. All his life Theseus had seen it in the eyes of women. If anyone had asked him, 'Theseus, do you know what love is?' he would have shrugged and said, 'Of course. Women have loved me all my life.' And who could blame him? Until Phaedra came to Athens, Theseus had never been in love.

Phaedra was . . . Phaedra was as lovely . . . Phaedra was as lovely as a woman can be (except those like Hippolyta who are lovely in nature as well). She did not sigh at the sight of him. She did not tremble at his touch. Her eyes did not linger lovingly on the back of his head after he had passed by. Little by little, this strange behaviour—quite unknown to Theseus—fascinated him. Finally he spent all his days wandering about Athens in the hope of catching sight of Phaedra.

He invited her to eat at the palace whenever she wanted, and once in a while she did. But whenever

Theseus sat down beside her, she lowered her eyes and left her food uneaten.

In the end, his passion grew to such a heat that he seized hold of her in the street and shouted, *'Why don't you like me, Phaedra?'*

Phaedra lowered her eyes and straightened her robes. 'My lord, you mistake me completely. Why should I not like you. I, not like Theseus? The glory of the world?'

'Well then, why don't you love me?'

'My lord, what love can there be between a king and an honourable maiden, without injury to her honour?'

'I'm not married. *You're* not married. Why shouldn't we marry? I'll make you queen of Athens!'

'What about Hippolyta?' asked Phaedra softly.

'What about her? I never married her exactly. She's a foreigner, isn't she? She's black. I won her in time of war . . . But you would have to take Hippolyte for your son. I want him to rule in Athens after me. Does that upset you?' He gnawed his lip in terror that Phaedra would refuse him.

But she raised her face, looked deeply and earnestly into Theseus's eyes and said, 'My lord! I would have it no other way. Hippolyte is a dear boy.'

When Theseus saw how he had won Phaedra, how at last he had won her, he gave a great leap in the air and spread his hands towards heaven as if to say, 'Thank you! Thank you, you immortal gods!' He did not even notice when the breeze set all the doors in the street banging, and brought up from the harbour the noise of tinkling shackles in the ships' rigging—a noise very much like laughter. Neither did he notice that Phaedra's eyes were different from the eyes of other women.

They were empty of love.

A band of musicians with curling horns went ahead of the bride and groom, and the route to the temple of Athene was strewn with flowers though the hot sun had shrivelled them by noon. Priests and priestesses chanted in harmony, and plumes of fragrant smoke rose from every altar, like the spiral columns of Knossos Palace. Dancers capered about with masks on poles in front of their faces—dolphins and mermaids, horses and lions—ducking and weaving between the guests.

The ruler of every petty province, the general of every military garrison in the region, the wife of every man of rank was there to see the wedding conducted with due ceremony. In fact everyone who could be paid or commanded to attend was present in the procession. Only the townspeople showed some unwillingness to go to the temple, but stood just inside the doors of their houses as the bride and groom went past. Few seemed to smile. The occasional voice shouted out, 'Hippolyta! Where's Hippolyta?'

Neither did little Hippolyte go to the wedding. Too young, said Theseus. Too little to remember it.

The dancing stopped. The hubbub was still. Phaedra and Theseus faced each other in front of the high priest. 'In the sight of Almighty Zeus, father of the gods who took Hera from among the ranks of the Immortals to be his wife, I, Theseus, king of Athens, take Phaedra to be mine, being an unmarried man and she an unmarried . . . '

'Is *that* what you are?' said a voice almost drowned by the banging-to of the temple doors. Hippolyta, dressed not in her Athenian robes but in only the skin of a lioness and carrying a clutch of spears, stood with her back to the door. First there was a craning of necks, then a murmur of astonishment and dismay, then a pushing and shoving as the congregation made way for Hippolyta. Phaedra, too, slipped her hand out of Theseus's hands and moved away into an angle of the wall.

'What do you want, Hippolyta?' said Theseus, and was surprised to find that his voice shook.

'What do I want?' said Hippolyta. 'What do I want? Justice. What do I want? Revenge. What do I want? My son. What do I want? Blood!' And she hurled one of her spears directly at Theseus's head. He ducked one, but to avoid the second he had to fling himself to the ground, and roll under a bench to shelter from the third.

'Someone give me a sword!' he yelled. 'What, are you all paralysed? Somebody give me a weapon!'

But there were no weapons worn in the temple of Pallas Athene, and the guests stood blinking and helpless.

On his back Theseus lifted the bench that was sheltering him, and hurled it at Hippolyta so that she was forced back down the centre aisle.

'What have I done, Hippolyta?' he said, trying to struggle to his feet. His sandals slipped on the marble and he did not succeed. He had nothing left but words to deflect her spears. 'I never thought *you* would turn on me like this!'

'You never thought? No! When did you ever *think*, except about Theseus? Theseus's glory. Theseus's victory. Theseus's happiness. Theseus's wife! I was a queen once—as powerful and victorious as you. But I *thought* you loved me, and I know I loved you. And I thought that that made you my husband and me your wife. I thought when Hippolyte was born that I was all the wife you would ever need. But no! You *thought* Hippolyta was a trophy you had won with a kiss and a string of clever words. Shame on you, Theseus! Shame on you for a spoiled child!'

She came on, lifting her black feet as she had lifted them once over twigs and stones and adders remorselessly stalking her prey. Her outstretched spear touched Theseus's collar-bone, the tip pressing then piercing the skin. Theseus looked down in astonishment at the tiny trickle of blood. 'You've wounded me, Hippolyta!' he said in disbelief. 'I'm bleeding.' He struggled to pull away from the pressure of the spear. 'I thought you loved me. I thought everybody loved me!'

'Ah, but love is a hawk, my darling Theseus. Love is a hawk you carry on your wrist. It will fly for you, kill for you, and come whenever you call. But only while you feed it and speak to it gently. If you leave it to starve, can you be surprised if it turns on you and *tears out your blue eyes*!'

Putting both hands to the end of her spear, she raised it to strike Theseus dead where he lay. But in that moment, a sunbeam wandered across the floor of the temple and shone on the grey-gold of Theseus's hair and on the tears starting into his eyes in terror. Hippolyta felt love stir one last time in her heart, and before she could thrust it back down, it had betrayed her.

Theseus's creeping fingers found the first spear she had thrown lying on the floor, and he snatched it up, kicked her feet from under her, and caught her on the spear-point as she fell on top of him. 'Treacherous Theseus . . .' she whispered, then died.

They say that when there is something evil afoot in the jungles on the distant shores of the ocean, all the birds stop singing. In the temple of Pallas Athene, there was not a sound, not a voice, not a murmur, not a cry. The congregation melted away through side doors and passageways, and Theseus and Phaedra were left to walk back alone along the route of the procession: king and queen, man and wife.

11

The Gods Reward Theseus

*M*y dear Hippolyte,

    On this, the occasion of your twentieth birthday, I send you my greetings and pray to the gods for your happiness and prosperity. Although I am not your true mother, I feel just as tenderly towards you as your father, the king. And the whole world knows that Theseus loves you more than life itself. Death holds no fears for him, knowing that you will inherit the crown of Athens and rule after him.

    However, the gods will not permit me to let this day pass without telling you one small secret which your father has kept from you. I would not be doing my duty as a stepmother if I did not tell you.

    You must often have asked yourself: who was my mother? It is time to tell you. Your mother was Hippolyta, Queen of the Amazons. You do not remember her, do you? So beautiful. So popular. What became of her? Now, when you read this, I must beg you not to upset yourself, not to feel you have a duty to avenge her, not to think any worse of your father. He felt it necessary—and who but the gods can say he was wrong?—to MURDER your mother. He stabbed her with a spear, in the temple of Pallas Athene.

81

Please do not let this spoil your birthday. I remain your affectionate stepmother, Phaedra.

Queen Phaedra rolled the letter, sealed it with wax, and sent her messenger with it to Hippolyte's bedroom. When the servant had gone, she sat in front of a mirror, pressing her cheeks with the back of her fingers. They were burning with the thrill of what she had just done. 'Now die, Theseus. Die at the hands of your own son.'

Hippolyte stifled a cry and then ripped the letter in two. For a minute he stared at the two pieces, then held them back together and reread the letter twice, three times.

It was not true—the part that said he did not remember his mother. He did have a few shreds of memory, like a torn picture, of long, dark fingers and a smiling mouth, and eyes as black as his own. He had simply not realized that the woman he remembered was his true mother. That much he was willing to believe. But murdered? By his own father? By Theseus the Hero?

All Athens knew Theseus to be the bravest, most renowned, wise, and just monarch on the shores of the Known World. The story of how he had killed the Minotaur and Poseidon's great blue bull had spread throughout the continent: princes would come just to sit at his feet and copy the clothes he wore, the way he cut his hair, the way he buckled on his sword. During his reign, the city of Athens had been graced with buildings more beautiful than any elsewhere in Hellas. People spoke of history as 'the time before Theseus'. Kill a woman? Kill his own son's mother? It was unthinkable. It was a lie.

Phaedra had meant, like a god prising open a volcano, to spill the boiling lava of Hippolyte's rage. Hippolyte's revenge would erupt and engulf Theseus.

She succeeded in loosing Hippolyte's temper, but instead of swearing revenge on his father, he leapt to his feet and roared along the corridors of the palace to Phaedra's own chamber.

Hippolyte smashed open the door and saw Queen Phaedra, her half-fastened hair tumbling down out of startled hands. She backed away from him.

'Why? Why did you send it? What did you think I would do? Did you really suppose I would believe you? Theseus—the legendary Theseus of Athens—a murderer of women?'

'But it's true,' said Phaedra lamely, and her voice failed her. Her plot had gone awry.

Or had it? Already footsteps were running on the stairs and landing. Help was on its way. Theseus would very soon arrive to witness the scene. 'Very well,' said Phaedra drawing herself up to her full height and tossing her head. 'I wanted you to kill Theseus. What are you going to do about it? All these years I have waited and plotted, plotted and waited. All these years I have waited for you to grow strong and Theseus to grow weaker. Theseus is getting old. I can twist him to my purposes. So what will you do about it?'

With a roar like a volcanic eruption, Hippolyte gave vent to his temper. 'I shall kill you myself!' he vowed, and putting his hands round her throat, he forced her backwards across the bed. Her fingers clawed at his face, but his thumbs were on her windpipe, and no sound came from her but a clucking like a hen whose neck is being wrung.

Then a hand like a vice rested on Hippolyte's shoulder and his father's voice said in his ear, 'What? Would you murder my queen? You have condemned yourself to death, you treacherous dog!'

'Not me, father! She slandered you! She wrote me a letter . . . she . . . ' He let go of Phaedra, unmanned by the

83

look in his father's eyes. Never had he seen such anger: it equalled his own, except that his own had suddenly deserted him. He felt ashamed and foolish to be found on his twentieth birthday throttling his stepmother. Phaedra wriggled free and into the protection of Theseus's arms. 'He tried to murder me, Theseus! I don't understand! Unless . . . I didn't tell you . . . I didn't want to hurt you. But last week Hippolyte begged me to stab you as you slept—said he was old enough to have the crown, and that if I killed you, he and I would reign over Athens together! I wrote him a letter telling him I wouldn't—that I loved you too much. The next thing I know he comes bursting in here! And he put his hands round my throat and I thought . . . I thought . . . oh, Theseus, my darling! I thought I should never see you again!' Tears flowed freely then from Phaedra's eyes, and Theseus hushed and soothed her.

Hippolyte began to speak—'It's not true . . . she said . . . she wrote to me that . . . '

'You black spawn of a foreign viper,' Theseus snarled, the spittle foaming round his mouth. 'You unnatural, murderous abomination! You stain on the world's mud. With my bare hands I'll kill you!'

'Oh no, father,' said Hippolyte peaceably, holding up his two hands as if to lay them on the king, even in self defence, would be a traitorous act. 'We must not ever fight, you and I. Let us never put to the test which of us is stronger. I'm twenty, father. You're getting old. I won't fight you, father. Don't make me fight you.'

'Aaaaaaaah!'

Every soul in the palace froze at the sound of the king's cry. His son stared at him in appalled fascination. 'Aaaaaaaah! You gods on Olympus! Listen now to the man they call Poseidon's son! Listen to the slayer of the Minotaur! Listen to Theseus of Athens. It is true! This tapeworm I have fed with my love, this weevil I have sheltered in my heart, this traitor I have entrusted with all my hopes—look how strong he has grown! *Revenge me, then!* I am waning like an old moon. My muscles are stiff, and the gore the bull-man gave me aches when the wind blows. Look down from Olympus and do not suffer the scum of the world to overwhelm the glory that was Theseus! *In the name of all I have ever done: revenge me and strike Hippolyte dead!'*

Hippolyte, white with horror and trembling with dismay, reached out one hand and touched his father's mouth as if to stop the words being said. It was like reaching towards the jaws of a mad dog. *'Cursed?'* he whispered. 'Have you truly cursed me, father?' Then he leapt over the bed and out of the window, touching the ground only a few yards from his own chariot. In blind panic, he jumped aboard it, winding the reins round and round his waist as he whipped the horses to a gallop.

Out of the yard, through the streets of Athens and along the road to the coast the chariot thundered, and behind it a cloud of dust rose up so high that it was visible from the peak of Olympus.

In the halls of heaven, against the walls of heaven, the gods reclined on their couches and looked at one another with eyes full of eternal boredom. Around them, like motes in a ray of sunlight, the ash from sacrificial fires drifted up from altars on earth. Wishful prayers, like the sound of a draught through a small and unsealable crack, whined continually around the legs of their couches. And now and then, like a door banging in a wind, came the words of a curse uttered on earth in the name of the gods.

'Well?' said Zeus the Almighty. 'We all heard Theseus

curse his son Hippolyte. Are we to answer his prayer and throw down our doom on the boy's head?'

Dionysus crushed a peach in his fist so that the juice ran down into a beaker, then drank. 'It's the first time he's ever asked for our help.'

'He's got by well enough without us before,' said Hermes, preening the wings on his helmet.

'I remember how his mother used to pray for us to forgive Theseus his terrible pride . . . but that was a long time ago,' said Hera, threading a needle while, at her feet, the Fates were cutting out a black robe, with sharp pairs of scissors.

'He slaughtered my bull and my bull's calf,' said Poseidon. 'And people call him my son when he's nothing of the kind.'

Only Pallas Athene stood by the vaulting door of heaven and, resting her chin on the end of her spear, looked wistfully down at the white sprawl of Athens near the coast of the blue sea. 'The boy Hippolyte doesn't deserve to die,' she said. 'He's done nothing wrong.'

'But Theseus deserves it,' said Zeus with a note of finality in his voice. 'Let us vote on the matter of Theseus's curse.'

Lazily, indolently, the gods each raised a hand: the right hand for yes, the left hand for no.

'It is decided,' said Zeus the Almighty. 'Poseidon, I think I can safely leave the matter with you.'

Hippolyte turned his chariot on to the coast road, the cliff-top road. He glanced continually up at the sky, expecting at any moment a thunderbolt to hurtle out of the clouds. But there was no roll of thunder and only the scrape and rattle of pebbles where the undertow of retreating waves rolled them down the beach. No one followed from the city. At last, Hippolyte slowed his horses to a walk. 'The gods have seen how father mistook me. They turned a deaf ear to his curse. The gods are just. What was I thinking of to run? I should have stayed and made him listen to the truth about Phaedra. I shall write to him from Corinth. I must make him believe me. It's not as though he doesn't love me: he's loved me for as long as I can remember . . . until now.'

Out at sea, the undercurrents moved with silent power beneath the lilac sheen of surface water. Like sheets of different colours, Poseidon the Sea-Shifter, the Earthquake-Maker, tied them with an overhand knot, and the steady rhythm of the sea's rise and fall was briefly interrupted.

Hippolyte looked out to sea and saw that a dyke of water was heaping itself across the mouth of the bay—a barrow of water—a fold of glassy sea piling up cliff-high—a tidal wave. Hippolyte flicked the reins of his chariot, but thought, Surely up here on the cliff . . . surely they would not send the sea when I'm way up here . . .

The wall of water began to move inshore, the seabed lay exposed ahead of it, looking bald and littered. The wave itself was clean—clean like a glacier. Only one small black shape was balanced on its summit. Faster and faster it moved, always forming a crest but never breaking. Sea and land were set to collide—the cliff of water with the cliff of rock.

They shattered in a white explosion of chalk and spray that soaked Hippolyte to the skin. The wave also delivered up, on to the land, off the crest of the tidal wave, a massive, black dog-seal.

It was vast and ebony, and gleamed like a slug. And when it opened its mouth, the bark that came out of it was like a pack of hounds. It raised itself, on angular flippers, and heaved its black blubber over the gravel of the roadway. The horses in the chariot screamed with terror and bolted. Hippolyte spread his feet wide and braced his knees against the sides. Every time the wheels went over a rock, he was tossed in the air, but managed to keep his footing . . . until the wheel-hub hit a tree stump and shattered.

The chariot rolled, the horses shattered the shafts. They galloped on with renewed speed now that they were rid of the weight of bronze—and had only the weight of the driver to pull.

Hippolyte, tied round with his reins, was dragged face-down along the rocky cliff-top path until the exhausted horses stumbled over the edge and into the sea below.

No trace of Hippolyte was ever found, except for a smashed chariot, a place where the hoof-marks stopped, and another, further back, where some damp, flippered beast had dragged itself along the roadway before diving back into the sea.

News was carried to Theseus while he was still comforting Queen Phaedra with kisses and soothing words. He turned the colour of cold volcanic ash and whispered, 'Why, Hippolyte? I loved you more than life itself. You and Phaedra were the whole world to me.'

But the news brought quite a different colour to Phaedra's cheeks. She broke free of Theseus's arms, threw back her head, and laughed out loud. 'It's done! It's over! I'm free!'

'Free?' said Theseus, already afraid.

'Free of *you*, Theseus. Free of twenty years of pretending to love you and being the dutiful and devoted queen. It's not as I intended, of course: I meant for Hippolyte to kill you. But this is better: he was *more* than life to you, and I made you curse him to his destruction. My revenge is perfect!'

'*Revenge?* But what have I ever done to you?' Theseus

stammered, shaking her by the shoulders. 'You're the only woman I ever loved . . . I never wronged you!'

'No. But you wronged my sister. You did her a grievous injury, then boasted to gods and men about it.'

'Your *sister*?'

'Yes, my sister—Ariadne of Knossos—the girl you promised to marry and then deserted on lonely Naxos. You broke her heart and in return I've broken yours!'

Grief gave way to anger. 'I'll kill you. I'll kill you, Phaedra!'

'I expect so. But then the people of Athens will never forgive you. You brought about the death of your father and mother; you killed beautiful Hippolyta and cursed your son—who was more glorious than ever you were. One more killing, and the legendary Theseus will be shamed for ever in the eyes of Athens.'

It was true. When Phaedra was executed in the market place, no crowds gathered to watch. The people stayed at home and muttered among themselves or crept out after dark to daub insults and crude bulls in paint on the palace shutters. The shutters were never opened any more.

One day, King Theseus dressed before dawn, took a caique from the harbour and sailed out to sea—to an uninhabited island close by Naxos. There he sank the caique and built himself a verandah out of the wreckage, in front of a cave where he slept at night.

Sailors passing by in ships sometimes saw him sitting beside a fire on the beach, and hailed him and waved greetings. But Theseus was rather too proud to wave back.